W9-BWO-279

GOLDEN
girl

Golden girl

Mari Mancusi

Aladdin

NEW YORK   LONDON   TORONTO   SYDNEY   NEW DELHI

ALADDIN

An imprint of Simon & Schuster Children's Publishing Division

1230 Avenue of the Americas, New York, New York 10020

First Aladdin hardcover edition December 2015

Text copyright © 2015 by Marianne Mancusi Beach

Jacket illustration copyright © 2015 by Lucy Truman

Also available in an Aladdin M!X edition.

All rights reserved, including the right of reproduction in whole or in part in any form.

ALADDIN is a trademark of Simon & Schuster, Inc.,

and related logo is a registered trademark of Simon & Schuster, Inc.

For information about special discounts for bulk purchases, please contact

Simon & Schuster Special Sales at 1-866-506-1949 or business@simonandschuster.com.

The Simon & Schuster Speakers Bureau can bring authors to your live event.

For more information or to book an event contact the Simon & Schuster Speakers Bureau at

1-866-248-3049 or visit our website at www.simonspeakers.com.

Jacket designed by Jessica Handelman

Interior designed by Hilary Zarycky

The text of this book was set in Goudy Oldstyle.

Manufactured in the United States of America 1115 FFG

2 4 6 8 10 9 7 5 3 1

Library of Congress Control Number 2015933119

ISBN 978-1-4814-3763-9 (hc)

ISBN 978-1-4814-3762-2 (pbk)

ISBN 978-1-4814-3764-6 (eBook)

To my father, who sometimes left me at the top of the ski trail . . . but always waited for me at the bottom. You knew I had the ability to fly—and you helped me find the courage to spread my wings.

And to my mother, who, while not the biggest fan of winter sports, has a sweet summer heart that's always able to warm away the iciest of chills.

GOLDEN
girl

PROLOGUE

One Year Ago . . .

adies and gentlemen! Next up in the seventeenth annual Parent's Day Competition here at Mountain Academy, we have four very talented athletes competing in the snowboard cross event."

I rocked back and forth on my board, my fingers white-knuckling the starting handles, unable to concentrate on the announcer's words as I looked down at the spectators below. This was my favorite part of the race. The anticipation. The adrenaline surging. I could barely feel the bitter Vermont wind whipping at my cheeks and stinging my eyes.

Today's typically dank December weather was likely

making many of the parental spectators down below wish they'd signed their children up for ballet or soccer back in the day—instead of encouraging them to take up a sport that required standing outside in subzero temperatures for hours on end. And who could blame them? It was tough to applaud even the most impressive of performances when your fingers were frozen—even in gloves.

But to us it was all part of the game. Cold meant snow. Snow meant snowboarding. And snowboarding meant everything.

"In the second stall, we have Alexis Miller, a seventh-grade freestyle rider here at the academy. She's the daughter of legendary Winter X Games star Bruce Miller—our illustrious head coach—and she's already done her old man proud, placing first in the Vermont Junior High Snowboarding State Championships earlier this year. We at Mountain Academy believe this little girl has a grand—and hopefully *golden*—future in the sport of snowboarding."

The crowd tittered appreciatively at the Olympic reference, and my face flushed—though thankfully no one could see it under my helmet. *A golden future.* I could only hope he was right. Of course, I still had a long way to go before I'd qualify for an invitation to the US Snowboarding Team. But I was definitely off to a good start.

"Great. We're in the stocks with *Golden Girl*," muttered a girl from the visiting team's school two stalls down. "I knew I should have stayed in bed this morning. At least that way I could have faced defeat with warm toes and hot chocolate."

"Oh please," came the reply from the girl beside me. "She's not all that."

That would be Olivia Masters, daughter of Cy Masters, owner of Green Mountain Resort, the school's neighboring luxury ski resort. Her dad and mine went way back: frat buddies in college, teammates at the Winter X Games. Meaning Olivia and I had been thrown together since our playpen days, the parental units believing that, as their offspring, we should naturally bond as they had.

But, turns out, I don't exactly play well with self-entitled brats, and Olivia isn't too fond of classmates who can kick her butt in every competitive event. And so the whole lifelong-besties thing never did quite work out between us.

"I mean, look at her." Olivia continued, throwing

me a scornful glance, not seeming at all concerned with the fact that I was standing right there, overhearing the conversation. Another reason we wouldn't be braiding each other's hair and having sleepovers anytime soon. "She weighs all of ninety pounds. She'll blow over in this wind"—she gave the other girl a sly wink—"*if* you know what I mean."

I knew what she meant. All too well. The snowboard cross event was supposed to be a no-contact sport—no bumping or pushing other riders off track. But with four snowboarders recklessly racing down a steep, narrow course, lined with hairpin turns and crazy big jumps, people tended to fall. And sometimes not by accident.

"Yeah, well, this so-called wind would have to catch me first," I muttered under my breath. "And considering its recent performance, I don't think I have too much to worry about."

Olivia scowled. She'd placed dead last at Regionals the week before, later blaming an ankle injury she'd suspiciously forgotten to mention before the race. The crushing defeat had wreaked havoc on her current year's ranking and earned her the nickname *Slow*-livia among the other students.

So yeah, a bit of a low blow. But to be fair, she started it.

"You just watch yourself, *Golden Girl*," she growled, clenching her gloved hands into tight fists. "Everyone knows pride comes before a fall. And someday soon, you're going to fall. Big time."

"Is that a threat?" I demanded, feeling my anger escalate. I knew it was my fault for engaging in trash talk to begin with—something my father had always lectured me about. *Save your energy for the race*, he'd say. But still, sometimes Olivia made me so mad. . . .

She smirked. "Call it a . . . prediction."

Cute. "Well, you can take that prediction and—"

A hand grabbed my jacket sleeve, strong fingers digging into my arm and effectively cutting off my retort. I turned to find Becca in the stall to my left, throwing me a stern *Don't let her get to you* look. I knew she was right.

I'd met Becca my first day at Mountain Academy. She was as tall and broad shouldered as I was short and skinny. And when Olivia decided to inform everyone that I had cooties and they needed to stay far, far away? Well, Becca plopped herself down next to me in the cafeteria anyway. She even went so far as to share her chocolate milk—drinking from the same straw.

Needless to say, we'd been inseparable ever since.

I reached over and squeezed her hand, feeling my anger melt away. "Good luck, girl," I whispered. And I meant it too. Not that she had any chance of beating me down the mountain, but second place still came with a cash prize and could score her some positive notice from sponsors. Maybe a free board, a new jacket. "I know you'll do great."

"*You'll* do great," she assured me. "And once you've won it all, you can celebrate during your big date tonight!"

"Argh!" I cried, my stomach immediately twisting into knots. "Why did you have to go and say that?" Cam had asked me to the school dance two weeks ago, and I'd found it nearly impossible to think of anything else ever since.

"Seriously, if I crash and burn now, I'm so blaming you," I huffed.

"I'd be okay with that if it gave me half a chance of winning this thing," she replied, giving me a sad smile.

Ugh. I hated when she got all self-critical. She was an amazing rider. One of the best in the school. If only she could gain a little confidence in herself and her abilities. I knew being downgraded to "alternate" on the snowboard cross team had really knocked her for a loop at the beginning of the year so I tried to boost her confidence whenever I could.

"Oh come on! You have as much chance as—" I started. But the announcer interrupted me.

"And they're off in five, four, three . . ."

I gave Becca one last encouraging smile then crouched down, bending my knees, hands gripping the starting handles, ready for the snap. That was the key to the cross. You had to be first out of the gate if you wanted the best chance to win.

"Two, one!"

The gates slammed down and I threw my hips forward, pushing off and jolting out of the pack, pumping over the first few rolling hills as fast as my little body could take me. Behind me, I heard a crashing sound, followed by a cry of rage. I couldn't afford to look back, but I had a pretty good idea of what I'd see if I did. The girl from the visiting school—the one Olivia had pretended to bond with at the starting gate—face-planting into the snow. Olivia was such a brute. If she were anyone but Cy Masters's only daughter, she would have been called out for her bad behavior long ago—and maybe even kicked out of school.

I pressed forward, aiming for the fast-approaching banked turn. The trick was to enter high so as to gain as much speed as possible as you exited around the bend. But as I neared the bank, a shadow fell over me—another rider hot on my heels. I dared take a peek, praying it was Becca. But, of course, it was Olivia, her eyes narrowed and locked onto me, a defiant expression on her face. She shot forward, cutting in front of me at just the wrong moment, forcing me to dig in an edge and slow down, wasting precious speed. But it was either that or collide into one of the flags and wipe out completely.

Olivia was now in the lead—barely, but enough to make me nervous. Forcing myself to remain focused, I scoped out the terrain, searching for the best place to pass. As I shot down the mountain, I realized I had started singing under my breath. Not loud enough for anyone to hear, mind you, but just mouthing the words. It was a trick my mother had taught me long ago. A way to keep my nerves steady and my mind focused. In fact, whenever I was stressed—on the slopes or off—humming a favorite tune usually brought me back to earth.

I could do this. I could still make this happen.

Choosing my line, I tucked my body in tight and made

my move, heading directly for the first big jump. Get good air off this and I'd find myself so far ahead I'd be able to send Olivia a consolation postcard through the mail.

But Olivia, it seemed, had other plans for me. Instead of taking advantage of the lead and choosing a straight path down the mountain toward a first-place win, she swung to the left, cutting me off once again. Startled by the unexpected move, I flailed and almost ate it. What was she trying to do? Didn't she care about keeping her lead? Or was she really that determined to take me down?

Pride comes before a fall. And someday soon, you're going to fall . . . big time.

I gritted my teeth, attempting to find my line again as we went over the second series of rolling snow banks, regaining speed before the big jump. I caught Olivia looking back at me, probably disappointed I'd somehow managed to stay upright, despite her best efforts. I gave her a friendly wave, imaging her scowl deepening under her helmet. Childish, I know, but oh so satisfying.

I realized our back and forth had slowed us down so much that Becca had caught up, and now the three of us were approaching the first jump neck and neck. I readied myself for the launch, bending my knees, weight on my back foot, and board flat, preparing to hit with maximum velocity. Or at least the best velocity I could muster having been cut off and slowed down twice. The cross was all about speed—no fancy tricks necessary over the jumps. Sometimes I'd throw in something simple—a quick tail grab or method—to give the crowd a little show, but not today. Not with Olivia deeply entrenched in some kind of revenge game.

This had to be down and dirty and super fast.

We hit the jump at almost the same time, three boards popping into the air, and for a moment everything was silent and still. Then we were back on solid ground, and suddenly I was in the lead again, though not by much. We swept around two more banked turns, still neck and neck as we readied for the next big jump. The one that would—if I played my cards right—give me enough ground to comfortably win the race. I was singing louder now. No matter what, I needed to win.

Concentrating as hard as I could, I tucked down again—knees bent and board flat. This was it. The moment of reckoning. I couldn't mess this up. I narrowed my eyes, focusing on the jump's lip, ready to pop up and soar—

But just as I hit the lip, I felt a strong tug at my back. Olivia must have grabbed my jacket from behind, hard enough to yank me off balance. I hit the jump lopsided, twisting into the air and flailing my arms to keep my balance. But it was no use. As Olivia and Becca flew past me, I tumbled helplessly back to earth.

I hit the ground hard, cartwheeling down the mountain at breakneck speed. I opened my mouth to scream but was immediately gagged by a face full of snow, my helmet flying off my head as I desperately tried to dig my board into the packed powder. But I couldn't seem to find an edge, and so I kept going, gaining speed with every tumble.

There was only one thing that could stop me now. A big old solid oak tree, looming in my path. I could hear the spectators gasping in horror. I fleetingly wondered if my dad was among them and if there was any way he could stage a last-second rescue, like he used to when I was little.

But, of course, I was no longer little. And this was no minor fall. *I'm sorry, Dad*, I thought as I hit the tree, praying that at least Becca had won the race.

CHAPTER ONE

One Year Later

H i there! I'm here to drop off Alexis Miller?"

I hugged my jacket closer to my chest as Mom slid down the rental-car window and addressed the man sitting in the guard shack outside Mountain Academy's wrought-iron front gate. It was only November, but the temperature had dropped, and the wind swirled through the car, stinging my still-sunburned nose. I breathed in, smelling hints of snow on the horizon. Most people didn't believe you could smell snow, but you could. There was this sweetness to the air just before the first flakes started to fall. The forecasters had predicted at least twelve to fifteen inches tonight, and Mom had decided to cut her trip short in order to get back to eighty-degree temperatures and sunshine. After having been married to my dad for twelve frostbitten years, she'd say, she'd had enough of the white stuff to last a lifetime.

The gates creaked open and the guard waved Mom through, allowing us access to the long, windy road flanked by large oak trees that led to the main campus. We'd missed foliage season by a couple weeks, and the trees' once-colorful leaves had faded and fallen—now blanketing the road in corpses of beige. As the bright morning sun filtered through bare branches, peering curiously into the car, I slouched in my seat and slid on my sunglasses, missing the vibrant palm trees in Mom's backyard already.

Mountain Academy for Skiers and Snowboarders used to be a traditional New England boarding school—offering elite educations to children whose parents summered at Cape Cod and wintered in Saint Barts. And for a time it seemed that it would stay that way forever, mass-producing future lawyers and doctors and politicians from here to eternity and beyond.

But then, in 1969, the stuffy founder of this stuffy

institution was found dead—facedown in a plate of stuffing. It was Thanksgiving. (I couldn't make this stuff up.) And the school ended up being passed down to his hippie-dippie fool of a grandson, Irving "Call me Moonbeam" Vandermarkson, who had somehow, over the years, managed to avoid becoming lawyer, doctor, or politician, even after graduating (barely) from his grandfather's prestigious school. In fact, Irving had somehow managed to avoid choosing a career at all. Until this one was dumped in his lap.

But Moonbeam wasn't interested in running a boring old boarding school like his grandfather. After all, he argued, there were plenty of other places to go if you wanted to suit up in a blazer and tie and pad your college application with Harvard-friendly extracurriculars. Moonbeam wanted to run a school where kids could learn something more spectacular than fractions and fiction and filling in the blanks.

Like skiing, for example. Moonbeam's favorite pastime.

So he quickly ejected the school's then-current crop of future leaders of America and replaced them with a ragtag team of young but promising skiers, remodeling the place after one of those famous Russian sports schools founded in the 1930s. As you can imagine, the board of trustees was horrified! How embarrassing! The school's reputation would never recover after these scruffy juvenile delinquents with funny boots and sticks strapped to their feet began parading down its halls.

But, go figure, it turned out Irving Vandermarkson—dirty hippie and ski bum extraordinaire—was actually onto something. In fact, his disgraceful little ski boarding school became a raging success. Today, more than one hundred Mountain Academy graduates have earned a spot on a national team—with fifty-four of them competing in the Winter Olympics and thirty-nine becoming medal winners. The school went from being a total joke to *the* place to enroll if you were serious about your winter-sports career.

And I had always been serious. Until now.

"Do I *really* have to do this?" I asked for the umpteenth time since we'd gotten off the plane in New Hampshire. "I mean, why can't I stay in Florida with you this winter?" Hanging out with my friends on the beach, tanning and talking and flirting with cute lifeguards sounded so much better than freezing my butt off up here while trying to chase my dream for a second time.

Mom offered me a rueful smile. "I wish you could," she said, reaching over to pat me on the knee, while keeping an eye on the windy road, already slick with black ice. "More than anything. But I don't make the rules."

When my parents split up three years ago and my mom moved out of state, the court awarded my dad custody from September to May so I could continue attending Mountain Academy. This year, however, Mom had gotten special permission for me to stay down in the Sunshine State until I finished my physical therapy. But now the doctors had given me a clean bill of health, leaving me no other choice but to trek back to the frozen tundra for the remainder of the winter.

I'd tried to argue that I'd rather walk over hot coals in bare feet while listening to Justin Bieber songs on an endless loop than return to this place. While Mom certainly sympathized, there was nothing she could do.

"Here we are," she announced unnecessarily, forcing perkiness as she pulled the rental car up to the front entrance of the school. Like most fancy New England boarding schools, Mountain Academy boasted a red-brick facade, complete with the requisite Ivy League ivy withering on the walls. I used to think it looked pretty cool. Like an old Victorian mansion from one of my mother's beloved Jane Austen books. Now it resembled a prison.

I dragged myself out of the car, my legs feeling like lead, and walked around to retrieve my suitcase from the trunk. Most of my stuff was already here, stored at my dad's place, a little staff cabin a few yards from the boys' dorm. I used to live there with him, but last year, after much begging and pleading, he'd allowed me to move into the girls' dorm like everyone else. Which, at the time, had been a dream come true. Now, however, the idea of facing all the curious stares and pitying looks from the student body—not to mention the smug smile of my archnemesis, Olivia, herself—made me wish I could hide out in his cabin for the entire winter.

As I yanked the suitcase from the trunk and started lugging it toward the school, Mom scurried after me. "You sure you don't need help with that?" she asked, her eyes falling worriedly to the bag in question. Something she would have never asked me, I realized, before my accident.

"I'm fine," I muttered.

"Okay, okay," she agreed quickly. Too quickly—as if she'd realized what she'd implied and felt bad about it. She grabbed me by my shoulders and pulled me into a big hug.

"I'll miss you, baby," she whispered in my ear.

"I'll miss you too, Mom."

"You're going to be fine. Really. It won't be as bad as you think."

I squirmed away.

"I'm serious, Lexi. . . ." Her voice drifted off, and I could tell she was searching for something positive, and, of course, completely cliché to say in a vain attempt to make me feel better. Like how I should get right back on that horse. Or time heals all wounds. Or I should turn lemons into lemonade. Or maybe the most ridiculous one of all: *It doesn't matter if you win or lose; it's how you play the game.*

Yeah right. Tell that to the Olympic committee.

"It's okay, Mom." I tried to reassure her. "I'll be fine. Promise." I gave her my biggest, best fake smile. The one I'd been using all year long to satisfy concerned aunts and uncles and doctors and friends. The one that said, *I'm fine.* Even though I wasn't.

Mom met my eyes, as if not fooled for a second. Then she sighed and planted a kiss on my nose like she used to do when I was little. "I know you will. You're my strong girl," she whispered, giving my shoulders a comforting squeeze. "My little warrior princess."

She started back to the car, then stopped. I watched her turn back slowly, her face a mess of mixed emotions. "Just . . . ," she started, then trailed off.

I furrowed my brow, wondering what she wanted to say. "Just what, Mom?" Was she finally going to tell me? Admit what I'd overheard the doctor say when he thought I wasn't listening? *She'll be able to snowboard again*, he'd told her. *But she may never be what she was before the accident.*

Which, in doctor speak, roughly translated to: *You know those silly little Olympic dreams? Yeah, not going to happen. Not in this lifetime anyway.*

Mom was silent, and I could practically see her warring thoughts battling one another inside her head. Then, at last, she sighed. "Just don't let him push you," she said in a quiet voice. "Trust your instincts. Go at your own pace. You have nothing to prove to anyone. Even if . . ." She trailed off again, and I knew she didn't want to say out loud what we both knew could be true. "You're special," she amended. "No matter what. Never forget that."

Oh great. I could feel the lump rise to my throat. The tears well up in my eyes. I'd promised myself I wouldn't cry. Not here. Not where someone could see. So I swallowed down the lump and swiped away the tears, forcing myself to nod my head.

"I've got to go," I mumbled, grabbing my suitcase and turning to head toward the dorm. I could feel Mom's eyes on my back, watching as I stumbled under the main archway leading into campus, unable to help but catch the familiar school quote above me, etched in stone and echoed by teachers and coaches all over school.

What would you attempt to do, it asked, *if you knew you could not fail?*

I used to love that quote. I used to say it all the time. Wrote it in notebooks, stickered it to my board. The same board that had cracked in two that fateful December day when I learned the truth.

That I could indeed fail. And that failure really hurt.

CHAPTER TWO

"exi Miller? Is that really you?"

My roommate Caitlin rushed me as I pushed open the door to our shared dorm room, throwing her fishnet-clad arms around me and squeezing me with wild abandon. In an instant I found myself tangled in a mess of black hair, red corset, plaid skirt, and Demonia platform boots.

"Whoa! Watch the ribs!" I protested with a laugh. As usual, even my miserable mood was powerless to resist her over-the-top exuberance. "Geez. It's too bad you're not excited to see me or anything."

She pulled away from the hug, searching my face with sparkling, kohl-rimmed green eyes. "Are you kidding?" she cried. "I've been counting the milliseconds.

It hasn't been easy, you know, keeping your bed safe for you. It's like everyone hates their roommate this year. Brooklyn even offered me a hundred bucks for your spot after she and Stinky Susan got in a fight over Susan's so-called lucky socks."

I wrinkled my nose. Susan was a good skier, but her unyielding belief that common, everyday soap could somehow wash away her competitive edge made no one very eager to get up close and personal—especially when she was on a winning streak. It wasn't surprising Brooklyn was willing to shell out the big bucks to save her olfactory glands, and I was grateful to Caitlin for standing strong under pressure.

"Brooklyn says she's actually glad she got her nose broken during the fight, because it's harder to smell Susan now." Caitlin shuddered. Then she grinned. "But enough about them. Let's talk about you. My wonderful, amazing, roommate extraordinaire—always Tide fresh and totally fabulous!" She released me and bounced over to her bed, which was clad in her favorite *Corpse Bride* bedspread. "Did I mention I'm soooo happy to see you?"

I shook my head with amusement as I wheeled my suitcase over to the empty side of the room. It was nice to feel welcomed back, even though I knew Caitlin would likely show the same level of enthusiasm over the news that the caf was serving pizza for lunch. That was just her—bright sunshine wrapped in gloomy paper. It was funny, most of the other goth girls I'd met were always so dark and depressed, bemoaning their tragic lives in suburbia and their boring, yuppie parents who didn't understand them. But Caitlin, though she loved the dark fashion and music, evidently had never gotten the misery memo. To her, life's cup was not only half full, it was overflowing with awesomesauce.

This was the second year I'd be rooming with Caitlin, since Becca's parents had paid for a single, insisting their daughter needed extreme quiet to study. Of course if they knew how little time Becca actually spent hitting the books, they'd probably ask for a refund.

I'd swung by Becca's room on the way up here, but it was empty—she must have been in class. Hopefully, I'd be able to find her at lunch. I felt like I hadn't talked to her in ages, and I missed her dreadfully. It was my fault, I guess. When I'd first gotten to the hospital, I'd been so depressed I refused all visitors. And by the time

I'd become more social, her parents had shipped her down to the Patagonia ski camp in Argentina for summer training, where she had no cell phone or computer access. She did text me when she got back—to find out whether I'd be in school this semester. At the time I wasn't sure. And by the time I did find out I was definitely coming back, I decided it would be fun to surprise her instead. I couldn't wait to see the look on her face when I waltzed into the cafeteria this afternoon. She was going to completely freak out!

I hoisted my suitcase onto the bed's bare mattress, realizing I'd need to grab some sheets at Dad's place before bed. Caitlin watched me curiously as I unzipped the luggage and pulled out a pair of jeans, placing them in the nearby dresser.

"I hope that side is okay," she said after a pause. "I did try e-mailing you at the beginning of the semester to see if you had a preference. . . ." She trailed off, her cheerful face wavering a bit. "But maybe I had your address wrong."

She hadn't, of course. I'd gotten her e-mail. I simply hadn't known what to reply. As with Becca, I didn't know at the time if I'd be coming back at all. If I'd ever snowboard again. But the idea of putting that in an e-mail . . . written down. As if it were already a fact . . .

"Sorry," I muttered, hanging a sweater in my closet. "I was pretty busy with"—my mind flashed guiltily to my lazy days lying out on the beach with my friends—"with therapy." I finished lamely.

"Oh!" Caitlin's eyes widened. "Right! Of course! I'm sorry. I didn't mean—" She suddenly looked as if she were about to cry. Great. I closed my suitcase, no longer feeling in the mood to unpack. This was exactly why I hadn't wanted to come back here. To face all the questions, the curious stares, the pitying eyes . . . all wondering if Golden Girl had finally lost her luster.

Time for a major subject change. "So . . . ," I started. "Have you seen Cam around? Is he as cute as ever?" Because of my accident, we never did get to go on our date. But now that I was back, I was more than ready for a rain check. After all, I might have hurt my knee. But my lips were working just fine.

"Um." Caitlin surprised me by hesitating. I watched her bite her lower lip. "I don't know if he's all *that* cute. And, to be honest, he's not all that smart, either, you know. In fact, I'd say he's kind of a—"

I frowned. "Caitlin, what are you trying to say?"

My roommate threw me a tormented look. "He's dating some new girl named Tera," she blurted out after a deathly long pause. "They've been hanging out for at least two weeks now."

I sat carefully on my bed. Two weeks? I'd missed my chance with the potential love of my life by two short weeks?

"But trust me, the girl's got nothing on you," Caitlin insisted loyally. "She's not half as pretty. And I heard she only got into school because her dad donated, like, some kind of library or something. She's not even that good of a skier."

But she was probably a great kisser.

"Well, it's for the best," I replied, trying to muster up some bravado as I pushed down the lump in my throat. "I have a lot to do this year. I wouldn't have much time for dating."

"Right." Caitlin nodded encouragingly. "Exactly! Who has time for boring old boys anyway? You've got the Olympics to qualify for." She grabbed me by the hand and dragged me off the bed. "Come on. It's lunchtime and the gang is all excited to see you. And bonus," she added with a super-wide grin. "There's pizza on the menu."

The Mountain Academy cafeteria wasn't like your typical high school caf, serving nasty dried-up chicken nuggets and shriveled Salisbury steak. After all, good nutrition is super important for snowboarders and skiers who, on average, can burn up to a thousand calories an hour while in hard-core training mode. So the school hired special nutritionists to create elaborate, healthy, calorie-rich menus and brought in five-star chefs to prepare each meal. It's one of the reasons tuition is so expensive here. We eat well.

I kept my head down and my hood up, attempting to keep a low profile as I followed Caitlin through the windy maze of tables on our way to our traditional lunch spot. We'd sat at the same table for years, ever since Becca and I first claimed it back in fifth grade. It was a sweet spot, overlooking the caf, while remaining close enough to the food line to make it easy to go back for seconds, as we often did.

I scanned the table as we approached. With the exception of Becca, the gang was all there, all talking animatedly to one another as they scarfed down plates piled sky high with food. On the left end sat Jennifer and Jordan, identical-twin alpine skiers who did everything together. Then there was Brooklyn to their right, who still sported a bandage on her nose from the aforementioned Stinky Susan incident. Next to her lounged Caitlin's best guy friend, Dante, the scruffy gamer geek who preferred virtual shredding to real life. As usual, his nose was buried in his phone and the Crazy Snowboard game app, pretending the rest of his tablemates didn't exist. Across from him sat Jessie, who was sketching on her napkin. She was a quiet artist who painted beautiful mountain landscapes that hung on the walls of several Mountain Academy classrooms. On the surface she appeared to be sweet and serene. But I knew she was an absolute monster on the half-pipe.

"Look who's here!" Caitlin squealed, slapping me on the back. Four out of the five pairs of eyes looked up (Dante kept his on his game), and suddenly I found myself drowning in a sea of excited chatter and questions.

"Where have you been?"

"When did you get back?"

"How's your leg?"

"How's your knee?"

"Are you totally better?"

"Are you back for good?"

I sucked in a breath, attempting to keep my composure. I tried to remind myself that they were being nice. Concerned about my well-being. They didn't know how much I didn't want to get into anything. I snuck a quick glance around the caf, looking for Becca, but came up empty.

"You should see the new park they built!" Jessie cried, dropping her pencil to grab her iPhone. She pulled up a photo and held it out for me to see. "They're calling it the Apocalypse."

"Yeah, it's slamming," agreed Dante, looking up from his game for the first time. "You're going to *die* when you see it!"

Out of the corner of my eye, I caught Caitlin giving him a warning look. His face paled.

"Oh, I didn't mean— I mean—" he stammered. "Well, you know what I meant." He shook his head, dropping his eyes back to his phone, his cheeks burning.

"Ignore him," Caitlin said, rolling her eyes. "The video games have rotted his brain."

"It's okay," I assured her, more than ready to change the subject. "I'll get him back tonight in the lounge when I crush him in Call of Duty." I turned to Dante. "Hope you've been practicing, gamer boy. Being stuck in a cast has given me much time to hone my mad skills." I threw out some made-up gang symbols and everyone laughed. Even Dante looked up from his game with a chuckle.

"You're so on, Golden Girl."

"Watch out Mountain Academy!" Brooklyn piped in. "Our Lexi is *back*!" She grinned, raising her hand to fist-bump me. "Back like a heart attack!"

CHAPTER THREE

Everyone cheered again, and I accepted several more fist bumps and high fives before they went back to their food, leaving me standing there like a grinning fool, wondering how long it would take for them to discover the truth. That while I had no fears of being bested in any video game, getting back on the real-life mountain, after a year away, was going to be a bit more of a challenge. *Back like a heart attack?* More like I was probably going to *have* a heart attack my first trip down a double black diamond.

But how could I admit something like that to a tableful of Olympic hopefuls? Sure, it was one thing to tell my Florida friends. They figured things were cool as long as I hadn't injured my flirting muscle and could still achieve a golden tan. But to a Mountain Academy student a lost Olympic dream might as well have been a death sentence.

I shuffled from foot to foot, feeling awkward as anything. "I, uh, need to get some lunch," I announced at last, though truth be told I was no longer hungry. As I retreated to the soup line, Caitlin chased after me.

"Sorry," she said, looking sheepish. "I told them to be cool. But you know how they are. Especially Dante."

"They were fine," I assured her, not wanting to get into it. "Even Dante." I gave her one of my fake smiles. "Seriously, don't worry about it. It's all good."

"Yay!" she cheered, grinning from ear to ear, completely buying my act. "I so missed you!" she squealed. "I really did!"

I sighed. "I missed you, too." I glanced back at the table to see if Becca had arrived yet, but it didn't look like it from here. Where was she? She was completely ruining my surprise! Not to mention she was the only one I could really, truly talk to about this kind of stuff. I seriously needed to find her and fast, or I was going to go insane.

The line moved, and a few minutes later we stepped

up to the counter, where a familiar face was ladling out several different types of soup.

"Hey, Mrs. Conrad." I greeted her, placing my tray down in front of my favorite cafeteria lady. I breathed in, enjoying the rich, warm smells wafting from the cauldrons. "How's it going?"

"Lexi Miller?" she cried, her mouth dropping open in surprise. "I haven't seen you all year!" She gave me a mock accusing look. "Have you been skipping the soup line and going straight for the pizza?" She wagged her finger playfully. "I shouldn't have to remind you of the importance of proper vegetables. . . ."

I held up my hands in innocence. "Come on, Mrs. Conrad! You know I'd never cheat on your delicious soup with a slimy piece of pepperoni. In fact, I just got back to school today. And the first thing I thought of was a big heaping bowl of chicken noodle."

"Well, that can be arranged." She smiled, her eyes crinkling at the corners. "It's good to have you back, sweetie," she said, reaching over the cauldron to give me a hug.

"Um, ew, do you mind? That's, like, completely unsanitary!"

We broke from the hug, and I whirled around to see none other than Olivia herself behind me in line. From the look on her face you'd think the poor cafeteria lady had grabbed a pile of rat fur and thrown it into the soup on purpose.

Mrs. Conrad's face paled. "Sorry, Miss Masters," she murmured, quickly grabbing her ladle and pouring a steaming helping of soup into my bowl.

I scowled. With Olivia's dad running the food-services company at both his resort and the school, she believed it was her right to bully the staff anytime they broke some kind of imaginary Olivia food-safety rule. Especially staff members who dared be nice to her archenemy.

"Last week I swear I found a dog hair in my soup," Olivia continued haughtily. "I should have reported it."

"Are you sure that didn't come from your own head?" Caitlin asked sweetly.

Olivia's gaze swung in Caitlin's direction, then leveled on me, as if noticing me for the first time. I caught a glimpse of loathing cross her face—but she quickly masked it with a brilliant smile.

"Oh my gosh!" she squealed, bouncing up and down, turning to her little minions behind her. "Girls! Can you believe it? It's Lexi Miller! Our Golden Girl is back!" Before I could stop her, she threw her arms around me, giving me an enthusiastic, Caitlin-like hug. "Wow. Lexi Miller. I didn't think you'd be back this year."

I jerked away from the hug, my hackles rising. "Yeah, well, sorry to disappoint."

Her overly pink-glossed, bow-shaped mouth opened in a shocked O. "Disappoint?" she repeated, widening her big blue eyes in total innocence. "How could I *possibly* be disappointed to see you alive and well? After all, I was *so* worried about you!" She gave me a thorough once-over, as if trying to assess my current state of well-being. I had to admit, she looked sincere. But behind her, I could hear her minions snicker. "It was such a horrific *accident*, after all," she clucked, all mother-hen-like. "I couldn't even imagine." Then she looked up at me, with the biggest, blandest, most pitying smile known to humankind. "You poor, poor dear. I *do* hope you'll be back on your feet soon."

I squeezed my hands into fists, anger burning through me like a fire. I mean, how dare she? How dare she stand there, looking so sympathetic and sweet when she was the one who had done this to me in the first place? It was all I could do not to scream out loud—to let everyone in the entire cafeteria know what a cheater she was. How she'd gone out of her way to ruin my life. How she didn't deserve to even be walking through these halls.

But I couldn't do that, of course. I couldn't say a single, solitary thing. Because if the truth came out, it would destroy Becca's life. And any self-satisfaction I might get in the short term would be dwarfed by the lifelong damage I would do to my best friend.

I forced myself to unclench my fists.

Because, you see, though it was Olivia who made me fall, it was Becca who crossed the finish line first that fateful morning, winning the race and earning a coveted spot on the school snowboard cross team. She even scored two sponsors out of the deal who hooked her up with some pretty sweet new gear. In short, my nightmare was Becca's dream come true. And the last thing I wanted to do was to wake her up. I knew full well if I told the powers that be that Olivia had cheated, the race would be invalidated, and my best friend would lose everything she'd gained.

No revenge was worth that.

So I'd bitten my tongue when Olivia pranced into

my hospital room the day after the accident, offering sickening sweet condolences with wide innocent eyes. And I'd said nothing when the school's safety committee grilled me about the incident two days later. I'd kept my mouth shut during my endless physical therapy sessions, and I knew I'd have to continue to stay quiet now that I was back in school.

But Caitlin didn't.

"Oh, don't you worry, *Slow*-livia!" my roommate butted in, stepping between us like a protective pit bull. Her eyes flashed with challenge. "I'm sure you'll be eating Lexi's snowy dust in no time at all."

"Caitlin . . . ," I tried. The last thing I wanted was to start this all up again. I turned to Olivia. "Look, Olivia, I—"

But Olivia just waved me off, glaring at Caitlin, the revulsion back in her eyes. "I guess we'll just have to see," she growled in a low voice. Then she turned to her friends. "Come on," she commanded. "The reek of desperation has made me lose my appetite."

The three girls, none of who appeared to have been stricken by the same appetite loss, glanced longingly at the steaming cauldrons of soup and piles of French bread at the head of the line before reluctantly following their foodless leader back to their table. I gave Caitlin an exasperated look. Her face fell.

"Sorry," she blurted out. "She just makes me so mad. I can't help myself!"

I gave her a rueful smile and put my arm around her shoulder. "I know," I assured her. "I know. And I appreciate it. Just—let's not feed the trolls, okay? She's already nasty enough without you poking her on purpose."

Ugh. I so needed to find Becca. She was the only one who would truly understand. But where was she? As we headed back to our table, I realized she was still MIA.

"Where on earth is Becca?" I asked Caitlin. "Why isn't she at our table?"

A shadow crossed Caitlin's face. "Um," she said, gnawing at her lower lip. "There's something you should know about Becca. . . ." She trailed off, looking unhappy.

"What?"

"Well, it's just that . . . I mean you weren't here and . . ."

My heart thudded in my chest. "Come on, Cait. Spill."

Caitlin looked at me glumly, then nodded her head to the right. I turned to look, my mouth dropping open in shock as my eyes fell upon something I would have sworn I'd never, ever see in the history of sight.

Becca. My best friend, the one I'd shared everything with since I was seven years old, was currently standing with the Boarder Barbies. A clique led by none other than Olivia herself.

I turned back to Caitlin, my eyes filled with questions. My roommate shrugged. "She's one of them, now," she informed me.

Last year, before my accident, Olivia had formed this so-called secret club, which, of course, she then made sure everyone knew about. It was invitation only, and while I never did quite figure out what they did during their "secret" meetings, it seemed as if the club's sole mission was to make sure everyone not in the club was clear on the fact that they were not in the club for a reason.

Not like we cared. In fact, I remembered spending lunches with Becca, laughing so hard that food shot out of my nose as we made fun of the girls who would kiss Olivia's butt for the remote chance of getting invited to join her stupid club. We both agreed they were mindless little lemmings, ready to jump off a cliff for their fearless fashionista in a manner I previously thought reserved for bad teen movies.

So what in the world was Becca doing hanging out with them now? No, not only hanging out, but laughing out loud at something Olivia said. As if it were even remotely possible that my archnemesis could say anything the least bit humorous.

It was then that I noticed Becca's outfit. The tomboy who swore she'd never be caught dead in anything but a Boston sports team T-shirt and a pair of baggy jeans was currently dressed in a belted tunic top and leggings with sparkly flats on her feet. And was that actually lipstick on her lips?

"There's got to be some explanation," I said to Caitlin, trying to swallow down the bile rising to my throat. "Like, maybe she's there on recon? Finding out their pathetic little secrets to use as blackmail later on when she needs extra points at the snack bar?" My bestie did love herself a bonus bag of Skittles or two. . . .

But Caitlin shook her head. "She was recruited back in February," she explained, her normally cheerful face looking a little sad. "And she spends nearly all her time with them now. She even sits with them at lunch."

My heart sank. Ever since that first day at school, when Becca had shared her chocolate milk with me, the alleged cootie victim, we'd never missed a lunch together.

"Maybe it's just 'cause I was gone," I suggested, knowing I was starting to sound a bit desperate and ridiculous. "Maybe now that I'm back . . . ?" But even as I said the words, doubt started creeping through me. Suddenly I remembered all the times I'd tried to get in touch with her over the last year. She'd been busy or with no cell phone access or out of the country or could only talk for a second before dinner. All along I'd accepted her excuses—all of them—because we'd been such good friends for such a long time. But really, when was the last time we'd actually talked? I wasn't sure I could remember.

I watched as Becca reached out and poked Olivia playfully and laughed.

Could Olivia really have not only stolen my future— but also my best friend?

CHAPTER FOUR

There's my little Golden Girl!"

My father's eyes lit up as I pushed open the squeaky front door and walked into the repair hut after lunch, giving him a small wave. The place was a mess, just as I'd remembered it, stacked floor to ceiling with bindings and boards, lug nuts and leather straps, screwdrivers and saws. The folks at *Hoarders* would have had a field day. But that was my dad; always refusing to throw anything away. You never knew, he'd say, when the one thing you thought was totally useless would end up saving the day.

It was kind of comforting, in a way. To know that no matter what had happened, no matter how long I'd been gone, no matter how traitorous my best friend turned out to be, some things—like the ski and snowboard repair hut—would always remain the same.

Dad dropped the bindings he'd been working on and walked around the paint-smeared worktable, grabbing me in a fierce hug and twirling me around, as was his typical MO. He smelled the same too, and I found myself taking in deep breaths of Old Spice, already feeling a little warmer than when I first walked in.

"I just ate!" I protested. "You're going to make me hurl."

He laughed and set me down, giving me a critical once-over. I noticed a streak of salt and pepper at his temples that hadn't been there last year. I guess not everything could stay frozen in time.

"You're tanned," he observed, a hint of disapproval in his voice. I knew it had nothing to do with his concern over my future skin-cancer bills.

"Yeah, well, Florida." I shrugged. "What can you do?" Dad hadn't exactly agreed with the decision for me to stay down in the Sunshine State for two extra months, saying I could have found a new physical therapist in Vermont to complete my rehab. But Mom insisted. And she got the courts to sign off on it, leaving him little choice and a lot of resentment.

"Right." He led me over to two dingy plastic folding chairs across from one another, gesturing for me to sit down in the closest one. Then he headed over to the shop's kitchenette and set out to make me hot chocolate, remembering, I noticed, to use two packets, just the way I liked it. "Well, how was the trip up? You made it in perfect time—we're supposed to get dumped on tonight. The powder will be unreal for first tracks tomorrow!" He grinned widely. "Are you psyched to be back or what?"

I made a face. He knew that I wasn't. He had to know, right? How in the world could I be excited to be back after all that had happened last year? But Dad, as always, was the eternal optimist, living in his fun, fantastical, glass-half-full world where nothing ever went wrong. It used to drive Mom crazy—probably one of the reasons they split—but I used to love it. To Dad every goal was achievable, every star was in reach. Anything we wanted could be ours, if we just kept a positive attitude and weren't afraid to chase after our dreams.

Now I was starting to see Mom's point.

"You should see what they've done to the course this year," he continued, pouring hot water into my mug.

"It's totally sweet. You're going to break records for sure."

I squirmed in my seat. "Um, I don't know about *that*." I didn't want to rain on his delusional parade, but it couldn't be helped.

He stopped, turning to me, furrowing his brow. "And why not, may I ask?"

Seriously, did I have to spell it out for him? "Um, hello?" I waved my hands. "A little accident a year ago? Broken leg? Dislocated knee? Ring any bells?"

He gave me a grim smile. "Yes, I do seem to remember something like that. But I also remember the next day—my daughter promising me she'd be strapping on that snowboard again in no time flat. Telling me that no little injury was going to stand in *her* way of Olympic gold."

Had I really said that? "It must have been all the drugs they gave me in the hospital," I muttered.

"Besides, I thought the doctor gave you a clean bill of health," my dad added. "Your mom said you had permission to continue your training immediately."

"Yeah. But . . ." I trailed off with a sigh. I was so not going to win this fight, and I knew it.

"Look, Lex, no one's expecting you to go out there

and hit a double black diamond your first day back," Dad told me as he sat down in the chair across from me, pushing the steaming mug into my hands. "But if you still want to chase this dream, you have to get right back on that horse. That's what professional athletes do. They heal and move on. This is a new year. We're starting fresh, and we're not going to let some little, old, completely healed injury get in our way, now are we?"

Don't let him push you. Mom's words echoed in my head.

I stared down at my hot chocolate, no longer feeling like drinking it. I used to love how Dad would always say "we" when it came to my snowboarding career. Like the two of us were a team. That we were in this together—whatever might come our way. But now the implication only irritated me. *We* didn't crash into a tree. *We* didn't break our leg in two places. *We* didn't suffer through months of painful physical therapy to get back to where we once were.

You've got nothing to prove to anyone.

"Look, honey, I'm not trying to downplay your accident," he assured me. "It was a horrible thing, and I thank my lucky stars every day you came out of it in one piece. After all, I know firsthand what it's like to deal with a serious injury on the slopes."

I stifled a groan, knowing exactly what was coming next. That legendary story about how *he* qualified for the Winter X Games while suffering from a broken collarbone.

"Did I ever tell you about the time I qualified for the Winter X Games with a broken collarbone?"

My dad was nothing if not predictable.

I forced myself to slug down a mouthful of hot chocolate as he droned on, even though it tasted like mud. It was a story he'd told me a thousand times before. About him colliding with a fellow rider and ending up in the hospital. About evading the hospital staff and climbing out of a second-story window at first light—just so he could make it in time for the qualifying rounds of the event. About how, even in total agony, he managed to score his spot on the team.

A professional athlete, he would finish, never let an injury rob them of their dreams.

I wanted to mention that perhaps Swiss gold medalist Tanja Frieden might have disagreed, having had to retire from the sport in a wheelchair after tearing two Achilles tendons. But I knew Dad would just list ten other riders who had pushed through broken ribs, busted knees, and crippling concussions. Snowboard cross was the most dangerous sport in the Olympic Games, and I had always known it. But it was one thing to know you could get hurt. Quite another to actually feel the pain.

You're special, no matter what.

Dad rubbed my head, messing up my hair, his eyes shining with affection. "I know it's scary," he told me. "But we're going to get through this. I'll be by your side the entire way. We're going to have a terrific year. And by the end of this month, I guarantee you're going to be saying 'What accident?' as we start winning races and racking up the points toward our nomination for Team USA."

I sighed. It was what I'd always wanted. The *only* thing I'd *ever* wanted. And Dad had done everything in his power to get me to this point. The hot chocolate churned in my stomach as I stole a glance at his hopeful face, begging me to agree with him. To say I'd keep going no matter what—so his sacrifices would not be in vain. Dad had given up everything to help me chase my Olympic dream. His job, his bank account, even his weekends—spent giving me extra one-on-one training instead of relaxing in front of the TV and watching football like other dads. And he'd never once complained about any of it.

So how could I give up now? How could I let him down? He didn't quit. How could I?

"Now, finish your hot chocolate and get out there," Dad commanded. "You're meeting your trainer in half an hour over on Baby Bear."

I looked up, surprised, my heart beating wildly in my chest as I digested his words. "What?" I managed to squeak out. "Today?"

"Yes today. Why not?" Dad gave me a surprised look. As if he couldn't fathom the idea of missing a single day out on the slopes. Which, of course, he couldn't. "We need to get you back in the swing of things as soon as possible so you can eventually rejoin your classmates." He paused, then added, "I told you this on the phone, remember?"

"Yeah, but I didn't know I'd be starting today," I protested, the prospect chilling me to the bone. I had figured I'd have at least a few days to settle in to life here before daring that first run down the mountain. I should have known better.

"Would waiting till tomorrow make that first run any easier?" Dad asked pointedly. "It's going to blow, no matter what, Lex. Better to get it over with."

I let out a long breath, knowing he was right. What good would waiting do? I'd probably only end up psyching myself out further the longer I stayed away. Maybe trial by fire was the best way to banish the fear from my head. And, like he said, it wasn't as if I was going to go hit a double black D. Baby Bear was the easiest trail on the mountain. A four-year-old could master it.

"Fine," I said, looking up. "I'll grab my board and go meet her. Thanks."

"Awesome," Dad pronounced as he rose from his seat. He shot me an affectionate grin. "You're going to do great out there," he assured me. "It'll be like you never left."

He was right, I told myself as I said good-bye and headed out of the hut and into the crisp afternoon air. I was perfectly fine. Physically healed. There was nothing to hold me back from regaining my Mountain Academy crown. To prove to everyone that I still had what it took to be a star. Sure, this kind of setback might have stalled your average Olympic contender's career. But I was Golden Girl. I was better than that.

So how come I still felt such overwhelming dread the closer I got toward the mountain?

CHAPTER FIVE

When people first hear "ski and snowboard school" they usually assume that all our classes take place outside and that we soar down the slopes from dawn till dusk without a care in the world for anything boring and educational. But, though most of us would probably prefer that kind of all-practice-all-the-time schedule, unfortunately the grand state of Vermont feels it's important that we athletes still receive a well-rounded education. I suppose it makes sense, seeing as the average winter-sports career has a retirement age of about thirty (without any retirement plan to speak of). Sure, the more accomplished athletes usually end up as coaches, such as my dad, or working the circuit as announcers or the like. But the rest? If they didn't manage to score enough sponsor seed money during their glory days, they needed a backup plan.

That said, we still had to practice. A lot. So to maximize our time out on the slopes during the winter months, we'd spend off-season (from September to mid November and April to June) on an accelerated academic track—getting in as much regular instruction as possible before that first big snowfall. After that, our classroom time was cut in half, and we spent the majority of our days in training. Which, by the way, could mean an hour in the weight room or a round of soccer just as easily as a session in the half-pipe. At Mountain Academy they worked on sculpting the total athlete. After all, you couldn't make those massive airs if you weren't strong in many different kinds of ways.

This year, however, I'd missed all that early-semester cramming, courtesy of Mom's Florida homeschooling, and I'd arrived right in time for the true winter season, where we'd spend the entire afternoon out on the mountain. My classmates were all out there now, somewhere, honing their skills on the half-pipe or in the terrain park, while I, myself, would remain on an independent study program with a private instructor until I was pronounced ready to rejoin my friends.

It felt strange being back on a chairlift, inching my way toward the summit while watching the tiny ant-like skiers and snowboarders glide down the mountain below. It was a Friday, November, early in the season, so the place was pretty quiet, with only a few retirees and locals dotting the trails. Once Saturday hit, the resort would be packed with weekend warriors, ready to get their shred on after spending a rough week slaving away in their offices. I envied them, in a way. For them, the sport was a simple pastime, and no one was counting on them to do anything but have fun.

I gnawed at my lower lip, my anxiety rising with the altitude. On impulse, I started to sing under my breath, like I used to when things got tense during a race, concentrating on hitting all the right notes, remembering all the words—forgetting everything else. To my relief it seemed to work, and by the time I got up to the top of the mountain, I was so into the song, I almost forgot to get off the lift.

I raised the bar as the chairlift slowed, unfortunately not enough to stop me from stumbling on the dismount, unused to the feeling of slick snow and ice under my board. My face flamed as the lift operator made a move to help me back up. I waved him off, thankful that, at least, he must have been new and didn't recognize me. Once I cleared the chairlift path, I undid my second binding and carried my snowboard across the flat, toward the green-circle trail Baby Bear—where I was to meet my private instructor.

"Lexi! Over here!" a familiar voice cried just as I'd almost reached my intended trail. I whirled around in surprise. I hadn't realized the new terrain park, the Apocalypse, was two trails down from Baby Bear. And I definitely hadn't realized that the advanced freestyle snowboard class would be meeting there this afternoon. And I definitely, *definitely* hadn't planned on being recognized by Brooklyn as I tried to sneak past them. Awesome.

I ducked my head and kept moving, hoping perhaps Brooklyn would think she'd mistaken me for someone else. Some random stranger who just happened to be wearing the same exact purple-and-yellow limited-edition Burton jacket I'd won at Regionals last year.

Um, yeah. Right.

"Hey, Lexi, come over and check out the new park!" So much for low profile. Now the whole class was calling to me. Reluctantly I changed my path and headed over to the top of the trail, where the students were sitting on the snow, waiting for their turn to drop into the park below. Including, I noticed dismally, Olivia herself.

"Lexi!" Coach Basil exclaimed, waving at me. "Welcome back!"

A former pro-snowboarder, Coach Basil had retired at age twenty-five to coach at Mountain Academy after a tendon injury cut short her winter-sports career. In addition to being our coach, she also taught drama and served as the den mother for our floor. We all liked her and would often end up hanging out in her room, listening to her extensive indie-music collection. Sometimes she even let us download the albums from her player, as long as we promised not to tell the establishment.

"Thanks," I muttered, my face burning under my helmet. "It's, uh, good to be back."

"And it's great to see you, of course," Coach Basil replied carefully. Then she gave me a hard look. "But to be honest, Lexi, I didn't think you'd be up here so soon. In fact, I was told you wouldn't be rejoining our class for at least another month. . . ." She trailed off, and I flinched at her pitying expression, desperately wanting to dig myself a hole in the snow and hide. I could feel the eyes of my classmates on me now, especially Olivia's. What was I supposed to say? That I wasn't rejoining the advanced class after all? That I was actually headed over to the bunny slope instead?

I knew in my head there was no shame in it; in fact, any normal person would think it was a smart and sensible thing to do—to take it easy and find my feet before jumping off the deep end. But my fellow students weren't normal people—they were total sharks, and any hint of blood in the snow would spark a feeding frenzy. After all, there were only limited spots on the teams, and I couldn't let them think for even a second that mine was up for grabs.

"Please! You know Lexi," Brooklyn butted in. "She just couldn't wait to bomb this amazing new park." She turned to me, eyes shining. "Lexi, I promise you, girl, you are going to fall in love with this thing. It is made of awesome."

I opened my mouth to reply, but Olivia cut me off. "It *is* awesome," she agreed in a most patronizing tone.

"But Lexi, are you *sure* you're ready to hit something so *difficult*? I mean, after all you've been through! Maybe you should take it easy for a while. In fact," she added brightly, "there's a great bunny slope just across the way. Maybe you should just *hop* on over to that instead." Behind her the Boarder Barbies giggled and nudged one another.

I didn't know what to say. This was getting worse and worse. If I turned tail now, headed over to Baby Bear as Olivia had suggested, I'd only confirm what everyone was secretly hoping. That I'd lost my edge. That the injury had ruined me. That my coveted Golden Girl status was ripe for the taking.

But if I said, no, that I'd planned to hit the park all along, well, then I'd actually have to hit the park. With no warm-up. And my entire advanced freestyle snow-boarding class watching.

I knew I should turn and go. After all, I shouldn't have to prove anything to them. They could think what they wanted—it didn't change anything in the end. But then I caught Olivia's smug smirk out of the corner of my eye. As if she knew exactly what kind of bind she'd put me in.

I made my decision.

"Are you kidding?" I found myself saying. "I'm totally here to conquer the Apocalypse. And all I can say is there better be zombies!" I pantomimed locking and loading my imaginary shotgun with as much bravado as I could muster.

My classmates laughed and cheered. Coach Basil frowned. "Hang on a second. I need to make sure this has been cleared by your coach—or at least your father— before I let you go." She reached into her pocket and pulled out her walkie-talkie. "Class, hang tight for a second."

She turned and walked a few feet off so we couldn't overhear her conversation. I could feel the eyes of the rest of the class on me. I knew if I was going to make my move it would have to be now. Once Coach Basil talked to my dad, it'd be back to the bunny slope and humiliation city for sure.

Quickly and quietly—so as not to attract Coach Basil's attention, I strapped my feet into my board. I'd had to buy a new one to replace the one I'd snapped during the accident last year. It was a little stiffer than my previous board, but that would only help me go huge on the jumps.

Once I was strapped in, I inched over to the starting gate and peered down at the park below. Wow. Dante hadn't been kidding—this park was killer. The biggest, baddest park I'd ever seen—with sky-high rainbow rails and huge tabletop jumps. Handrails, kickers, picnic tables—this park had it all. I would have loved everything about it before my accident.

Now it just filled me with dread.

No big deal, I told myself, trying to ignore the eyes of my fellow students glued to my every move as I prepared to push off. I'd taken breaks from snowboarding before—it was like riding a bike. Not something I'd ever forget. Dad told me to get right back on that horse— that holding back would only psyche me out and make things more difficult in the end. This was my chance to prove not only to them—but also to myself—that I still had it. That Golden Girl still reigned supreme.

All I had to do was hit one feature. A jump, a rail, something to show them I hadn't lost it completely. As I squared my shoulders and attempted to force down my fear, I worked to summon up the adrenaline rush I used to get from looking down into a park. Could I find that somewhere again, buried deep inside?

"Lexi!" Coach Basil's disapproving voice cut through the crisp air. "I just spoke with your father, and he said you were supposed to—"

I pushed off, her protests lost in the crunch of snow as I dropped in, heading toward the first rainbow rail. The wind whipped at my face, stinging my cheeks and making my eyes water, but I ignored the pain, focusing on the task at hand. All I had to do was pop up onto the iron railing, slide down it, then jump off. Maybe throw in a little trick—a tail grab, a 180 turn, something small. No big deal. A six-year-old could do it.

Well, if that six-year-old got up enough speed, they could. Which, for some reason, I was having difficulty doing—my legs refusing to obey my brain's instructions, deciding instead to dig the edge of my board into the snow, forcing me to slow down. By the time I reached the rail, I didn't have enough speed to launch onto it, and I had to totally bail, skipping the feature and heading farther down the mountain.

You're okay, I told myself. *You'll just hit the next one.*

Unfortunately, the next one in this case turned out to be a huge tabletop jump. The same kind of jump I'd fallen on back in December. Great.

"Lexi!" I could vaguely hear Coach Basil's voice from far away. "Stop right now! You're not supposed to be—"

I tucked my body in tight, forcing myself to hit the launch pad head-on. Clenching my hands into fists, I attempted to find both speed and courage at the same time.

But just as I reached the jump, my vision spun, throwing me off-balance. A dizziness crashed over me and my throat locked up—stealing away my breath. My knees buckled under me as I careened off course, flew up into the air, and face-planted in the snow. As my heart pounded in my chest so hard I was sure it would break my ribs, a scream echoed through my ears. It took me a moment or two to realize it was coming from my own mouth.

"Lexi!"

Coach Basil's voice sounded like it was coming from far away, muffled by a thousand layers of cotton. I shook my head, attempting to clear my vision as I swiped away the snow caked onto my face. I tried to sit up, only to find myself collapsing back onto the trail, my hands shaking hard enough to create a whirlwind of flakes swirling around me.

"Are you okay?" Coach Basil cried, her voice closer this time. I felt hands on me, helping me sit up. I was still dizzy, but my vision had started to clear. "Did you hurt yourself?"

Did I? It took me a minute to assess. But no, nothing seemed to be injured. Except, of course, my pride. Not to mention my hopes and dreams.

And my golden snowboarding career, which now had officially turned to tin.

CHAPTER SIX

S eriously, what were you thinking, Lexi? Hitting the hardest snowboard park in the history of snowboard parks your first run after your accident? That's crazy—even for you!"

Caitlin plopped down beside me on my bed, where I was currently curled up, fetal position, staring at the wall. Pretty much the same position I'd been in since early that afternoon, after being dragged down the mountain by ski patrol. Which, I might add, pretty much ranked up there with the most embarrassing experiences of my life—with my entire advanced freestyle snowboarding class getting an up-close-and-personal look at my apocalyptic defeat on the Apocalypse.

It was one thing to fall. That was humiliating enough.

But then—when I realized I couldn't get back up no matter how hard I tried? That was when I wanted to crawl behind a snowbank and never come out.

Instead I lay there, sprawled out on the hill like the saddest of snow angels, with even the idea of standing up on my board making me sick to my stomach. My hands were shaking, and I could barely see through my tears. Coach Basil had to literally unstrap the board from my feet, just to get me to move. All while Olivia and the Boarder Barbies watched from their perches above.

Pride comes before a fall, Olivia had told me that fateful day. She hadn't been wrong.

Seriously, what was I thinking—believing I could just pick up right where I left off before the accident, no big deal? It seemed crazy now that I thought back to it. The stupidest idea ever. But then I remembered their eyes, drilling into me. Olivia's self-satisfied smirk. I'd wanted so badly to prove I still had it. That I was still Golden Girl. Still number one. And so I'd let common sense take a backseat to idiocy and managed to prove the exact opposite.

At first I'd seriously thought the fall had triggered a heart attack. After all, I had all the textbook symptoms:

shaking hands, shortness of breath, aching chest, numbness in my left arm. But when I asked the nurse in the first aid hut, she only shook her head. "There's nothing physically wrong with you, dear," she told me. "You just had a panic attack. Probably post-traumatic stress from your accident last year. You need to take it easy for a while. Take your time getting back up to speed. Maybe try the bunny slope?"

A panic attack? I didn't even know what that was. At least a heart attack was something real. A physical reason for me to have crashed and burned in front of my classmates. I could have redeemed myself from my hospital bed. Brave Lexi who tried to snowboard with a broken heart. That sounded almost noble.

But no, according to some quick WebMD research, the cause of my epic fail was literally all in my head. And there was no quick fix for this kind of thing either.

Feeling defeated, I'd trudged back to the dorm, where I lay in bed for the rest of the afternoon. Ignoring my father, who called three times and knocked on my door twice. The last thing I wanted to do was face him—Mr. Broken Collarbone at the Winter X Games. I bet he never let a little panic attack keep him from the sport he loved.

"It's not my fault," I moaned to my roommate. "You should have seen the way Olivia was looking at me. Like she was going to tell everyone in school how I'd lost it if I didn't go and prove that I hadn't."

"Yeah, well, you sure showed her," Caitlin snorted. I groaned.

"That's it," I declared. "I'm never, ever leaving my room again. Seriously. Not even to eat. They can drag out my corpse when it starts to out-stink Susan's socks."

Caitlin rolled her eyes. "No way," she protested. "You do that and you let Olivia win. So you fell. Big deal. We've all fallen. Olivia more than most, I might add. The best revenge is to get right back out there and show her you couldn't care less. That it'll take more than some silly tumble to bring Golden Girl down."

She sounded almost inspiring. But I knew she had an ulterior motive for the pep talk. Namely, to convince me to accompany her to the student ice cream social that evening. She said it would be good for me to get out of bed and enjoy the DJ and dancing and make-your-own-sundae bar. Normally I would have been all over this kind of thing—but now I just couldn't bring myself to face all the other kids staring at me and whispering.

"You've all fallen, but you've all gotten up," I pointed out miserably. "I had to be rescued. Does that scream future Olympian to you?" I rolled over in bed, staring up at the ceiling. "Face it, Caitlin. My career is over. I might as well drop out and enroll in public school at this point. Give it all up for good."

"Yeah, cause *that's* a well-thought-out plan," Caitlin remarked wryly. "Seriously, Lex. Stop the pity party for one second and think about it. You suffered a major accident. And your brain needs time to recover too—just like your body did. So how about you cut yourself some slack here?"

I made a face. "Do you think Shaun White cut *himself* some slack?" I asked, naming the world's most famous snowboarder. "Or what about Jamie Anderson? You think she ever had a panic attack on a simple tabletop jump?"

"Yes, I do, actually," Caitlin proclaimed. "In fact, I bet she's had some pretty major panic attacks in her day. And yes, I believe even Shaun White himself may have fallen once or twice in his illustrious snowboarding career. In fact, I've seen the YouTube videos.

"But luckily for us," she added, "and the entire snow-boarding industry—neither of them quit the sport they loved because they were afraid of what people would say about them."

She popped up from the bed and grabbed her Skel-animals backpack, heading for the door. "Come on," she urged. "If you won't do it for me, then do it for Shaun and Jamie. Show them they ain't got nothing on you."

CHAPTER SEVEN

aitlin was right; by avoiding Olivia and her Boarder Barbies, I was only letting them win. And hadn't I already determined I'd never let them win again? Not that today's fiasco was a promising start, but still.

So I told Caitlin to go on without me, I'd meet her there. Then I forced myself out of bed, took a quick shower, and changed into party clothes, slipping snowboard boots on my feet in case the forecasted blizzard was still on its way. I headed downstairs and across campus to the student rec center, where the ice cream social was being held.

Mountain Academy was famous for its ice cream socials. They purchased the ice cream from a farm down the hill that made it by hand using milk from their own cows. So it was always super fresh and extra creamy. And that was only the beginning of the awesome. There was also the infamous toppings bar, jam-packed with every possible ice cream topping you could think of: hot fudge, marshmallow, butterscotch, M&M's, gummy bears, Oreos—you name it, they had it. And the best part? You got to serve yourself, meaning you could pile an inhuman amount of whipped cream on top—a virtual mountain of the sweet stuff—and no one said a word to stop you.

The snow had just started to come down as I made my way across campus. Light, fluffy flakes gently dusting my jacket. According to my Weather.com app, the true blizzard wouldn't start till around midnight. But when it did, it was meant to be a mean one—a real nor'easter. Hopefully, we wouldn't lose power in the dorms. That was always a pain, trying to study by candlelight.

Though at the moment, studying was the least of my problems. I reached the rec center, realizing my hands were shaking like crazy. As I wrapped my fingers around the doorknob and prepared to go inside, I couldn't help but imagine how the next moments would play out. In my imagination I'd step through the doors. The music would screech to a halt. Everyone would turn and stare. Then, after a moment of shocked silence, the whispers and giggles would erupt like a volcano, flooding the hall and forcing me to flee the scene, retreating back to my dorm room in shame. At least that's how this kind of thing usually played out in the movies.

"What do you think you're doing, young lady?"

I dropped my hand from the door, whirling around guiltily, though, of course, I wasn't doing anything wrong. My eyes fell upon none other than Olivia's father, Cy Masters, owner of Green Mountain Resort, fast on approach, a furious look on his jowly face. I took a hesitant step back as he lumbered past, seeming not even to notice me as he passed the rec center, his eyes locked on something ahead.

Make that someone. As I peered around the corner, I recognized Olivia standing over by one of the empty ski racks, dressed in an absurdly huge white fur coat and eating a chocolate bar. I watched as she looked up to see her father, startled, then dropped the candy immediately, as if it were a hot potato.

"Oh, hi, Daddy," she chirped nervously, her trademark

saccharine-sweet voice cracking at the edges. "I didn't know you were on campus tonight. What a great surprise."

Her father didn't answer, reaching down to pick up the discarded candy bar and holding it up for observation. He raised a bushy eyebrow at his daughter, and I almost laughed at the expression on Olivia's face. So busted!

"It's not mine!" she protested, her voice rising into a panicked squeak. "I was just holding it for a friend."

Her father walked over to a nearby trash can and discarded the bar. "How many times have we talked about this, Olivia?" he demanded. "An athlete treats her body as a temple. You keep filling it with junk food and your performance will continue to suffer. You're already third to last on the team. You want to get cut altogether?"

Olivia's face crumbled. "You know I'm doing the best I can."

But her father wasn't finished. "To think I was under the impression that this would be our year. Our chance to pull ahead, with Alexis Miller out of the running. But no, you're too busy hanging out with your friends and poisoning your body with processed food to take advantage of this opportunity." He shook his head. "And now

Alexis is back. And any chance you had to slip ahead is over."

Olivia's face twisted into a scowl at the mention of my name. "Please," she spit out, regaining some of her bravado. "You should have seen her on the slopes today. I *hardly* think she'll be a threat."

"That's your problem, isn't it?" her father shot back. "You hardly think! Alexis Miller is the best snowboarder at Mountain Academy—maybe the best in the world, in her age group. If you underestimate her for even a second, you'll find yourself in second place for the rest of your life. Is that what you want?"

"No, Dad, but—"

He shook his head, looking tired and defeated. "What would your mom say if she could see you now?"

Olivia's face went stark white, her words seemingly stolen from her lips. For a moment they just stared at one another. Then her father humphed, as if he'd proven some point, before turning and barreling off, his heavy boots kicking up quite a snowstorm in their wake.

Olivia watched him go, her face a tangle of emotions. Then she swiped her wet cheek with the sleeve of her fur coat and started plodding toward the rec hall.

I tried to duck away, but I was too slow. Her eyes fell upon me, a look of horror flashing across her face before she could mask it. She knew I'd heard everything. She opened her mouth to say something, then seemed to change her mind.

"I'm sorry," I found myself saying, at a loss for anything else.

But Olivia just lifted her chin up high and pushed her way past me into the rec center, not dignifying me with a response.

CHAPTER EIGHT

I considered heading back to the dorm. After my encounter with Olivia, the last thing I felt like was ice cream and dancing. But I'd promised Caitlin, and I knew she'd be beyond annoyed if I let Olivia get to me again. So, after giving my archnemesis enough time to make a proper entrance, I slipped into the rec center, ready for anything.

To my relief, the music stayed pumping, the student body kept dancing and eating—as if the talk of the school hadn't just entered the building. In fact, the few people who did seem to notice my arrival didn't show anything more than the usual interest. Go figure.

I scanned the dance floor for my roommate, wanting to tell her about my run-in with Olivia. But first I spotted Cam, arm in arm with some black-haired girl in a cranberry-colored dress. Tera, I guessed. My heart squeezed a little as I quickly turned away. No big deal, I reminded myself. It just wasn't meant to be.

Still, could this day get any worse?

It was then my eyes fell upon a more welcome sight. Becca, standing alone over by the sundae bar, without a single Boarder Barbie in tow. Finally! The perfect opportunity to make my move.

Heart pounding in my chest, I approached, not sure at all what I was going to say to her once I got there. Should I make some kind of icebreaking joke? An emotional plea? Or how about a flat-out question? Like, for example, how on earth did "Darth Olivia" manage to turn my best friend and ultimate Jedi warrior to the Dark Side practically overnight?

Any or all of those strategies might have worked, except for the fact that when I did finally reach my friend, my tongue chose to stop operating altogether. Instead, I found myself standing there like an idiot, unable to form even the least coherent sentence. In return, Becca stared back at me with an unreadable expression on her face, also seeming at a loss for words.

As we faced off in silence, I couldn't help but notice her outfit. A pink, frilly knee-length dress. Seriously, you could have bet me a million dollars and I would have sworn up and down that my tomboy friend would not have been caught dead in such a girly ensemble.

But times, they were a-changin'.

"Um, hey," I finally managed to spit out after what seemed an eternity. Not exactly the most eloquent of openings, but it was the best I could muster under pressure.

"Um, hey," she replied. "I heard you were, um, back."

You did? I wanted to scream. *Then why didn't you come talk to me at lunch? Why didn't you come visit me in the dorm?*

"Yeah," I said instead. "I, uh, arrived this morning."

We lapsed into more awkward silence as the DJ added a Beyoncé tune to the mix. Gah! Why was this so hard? This was my bestest friend in the entire world. The girl I'd shared everything with since I was seven years old. The girl I'd giggled with under the covers during sleepovers in my dad's cabin, long after lights-out. The one I'd told secrets to that I'd never told another living soul. Becca probably knew me better than I knew myself. So why did she suddenly feel like a complete stranger?

It was then that I noticed her fingers digging into her sundae bowl so hard, I was half afraid she'd poke through the Styrofoam. It was like she wanted to talk to me, but something was holding her back.

I decided to try another tactic. "So I hear congratulations are in order," I said, giving her a hesitant smile. "You made the snowboard cross team? And new sponsors, right? That's so awesome."

Her face turned bright red, and she stared down at her sundae, as if she wished she could crawl inside of it and hide. "Thanks," she muttered. "Though I'll probably drop back down to alternate now that you're back."

"I wouldn't be too sure of that," I replied, surprised she hadn't heard about my little performance on the slopes that afternoon. Surely Olivia hadn't missed an opportunity to relate to her entire crew the wild and crazy Lexi disaster tale. Maybe Becca was just being nice. "Besides, you're amazing. You know, even if I hadn't fallen, I bet you would have won that race anyway. You were on fire that—"

Becca dropped her sundae. It hit the floor, whipped

cream and hot chocolate splattering everywhere, soaking my pants. "S-sorry," she stammered, dropping to her knees to wipe up the mess. I could see tears welling up in her brown eyes as she grabbed scoopfuls of ice cream off the floor with her bare hands, haphazardly dropping them back into her bowl.

I stared at her in shock, realization hitting me with the force of a ten-ton truck. Was that it? Was that why things were so weird between us? Did she feel guilty that her career had taken off because mine had crashed and burned?

"Hey!" I cried, grabbing a handful of napkins and scrambling down to the floor beside her. I handed half the stack to her and kept half for myself. "It wasn't your fault," I reminded her, wiping down the cement. "It's just how the cross is sometimes. People fall." I wondered, not for the first time, if I should tell her the truth. That if anyone should feel guilty, it should be Olivia, not her.

But no. I couldn't do that to her. She might opt to do something all noble—like give up her spot on the team, deciding she didn't deserve it. It was much better to stay quiet and allow her to enjoy her new opportunity. After all, she certainly worked hard enough for it. And who knew? Like I'd said, maybe she would have won anyway, even if Olivia hadn't gone and sabotaged me. I had to go with that, for her sake.

I realized it was time for a subject change. "You know, it seems a waste to throw out all this good ice cream," I remarked casually. "You don't suppose the five-second rule applies in this case?" I grabbed a spoon off the table and dug into the now grime-caked sundae. Holding it up to my mouth, I grinned. "Come on," I teased. "Dare me."

Becca stared at me for a moment, as if in disbelief. Then she started to laugh. "Ew, Lexi!" she cried. "Gross! Don't you even think—"

"Oh, I'm sorry! Did you want it all for yourself?" I swooped the spoon toward her face. "Here comes the airplane, baby Becca . . . in for a landing!"

She squealed, swatting the spoon away. The ice cream went flying—

—landing on a pair of expensive-looking patent-leather boots.

Uh-oh. My eyes traveled up, from boots to black tights to plaid skirt to white fur coat. . . .

"Becca Montgomery!" Olivia cried, a disgusted look on her face as she stared down at me and my friend. She'd evidently hit the bathroom and reapplied her smeared makeup. Only a slight redness to her eyes hinted at what had gone down between her and her dad.

I watched as Olivia snapped her fingers, and one of the Boarder Barbies, a sixth grader by my guess, dropped to her knees, wiping the offending ice cream from Olivia's boots. I was half-amazed Olivia didn't make her lick it off instead. "What on earth are you doing on the floor?" she added, returning her attention to Becca.

"Oh," Becca cried. Her smile faded as she scrambled to her feet. "I dropped my sundae, and Lexi was helping me wipe up the mess." Ugh. She sounded so apologetic. As if she'd done something wrong. What happened to my kick-butt, girl-power bestie?

Olivia snorted. "Well, that's good for *Lexi*," she replied. "Practicing for her future venture in custodial arts, now that her little snowboarding career has come screeching to a halt." She grabbed Becca by the sleeve. "But you, Montgomery, have more important things to do. Ava's in the bathroom with a wardrobe malfunction, and you're the only one who knows how to sew."

"Excuse me," I interrupted, rising to my feet, anger flaring. I was so close to getting my old friend back—I just knew it. "Becca and I were in the middle of talking. Ava will have to wait."

Olivia rolled her eyes. "Well, I suppose we better let Becca decide that, don't you think?" She released her arm. "Well, Becca, my dear?"

I stole a glance at my friend. *Please pick me, please pick me, please pick me.* I swear at that moment I would have given up Olympic gold forever just to have my best friend tell Olivia to get lost. That she had her true friend back now and didn't need those brainless Boarder Barbies.

Becca looked at me, then at Olivia, her face a war of emotions. I gnawed on my lower lip, beginning to get nervous. What was going on with her? How could she even consider choosing Olivia over me?

"Becca, what's wrong?" I found myself asking, my eyes welling up with tears. I knew I shouldn't be acting this vulnerable in front of Olivia—it would only give her more ammunition. But I couldn't help it. "What's going on with you? Did I do something? Whatever it was, tell me and I'll make it up to you!" My mind raced for reasons that she could be mad at me, but I kept coming up blank.

Becca squeezed her eyes shut, then opened them, her face now a mask of resignation. "Sorry, Lexi," she mumbled. "I need to help Ava." And with that, she shuffled off in the direction of the bathroom, leaving me alone with Olivia, who was now beaming wider than the Cheshire cat.

It was the last straw. My body took over, ignoring my mind's plea to take the higher road. Instead I grabbed Becca's discarded bowl and shoved it into Olivia's face. She screamed as the grimy whipped cream and chocolate syrup dripped down her cheeks. As she tried to wipe it away, she only managed to get chocolate on her pristine white coat and gain the attention of the other students. Now everyone was staring at *her* in the way I'd first imagined them staring at me.

"You are so dead," she snarled in her most venomous of tones. "I will get you, Lexi Miller, if it's the last thing I do."

"Please. What could you possibly do to me," I shot back, "that you haven't already done?"

And with that, I turned and fled the party.

CHAPTER NINE

I f life were a movie, the cameras would be following me as I abandoned the rec center, stepping out onto the snow-dusted grounds on my way back to the dorm. Maybe I'd be stomping angrily; maybe I'd be shedding a few dramatic tears. Either way, the sound track would be gloomy and dark and hopeless. In the credits it'd be listed as "Requiem for a Friend" or something equally as depressing.

Then, out of nowhere, the cameras would cut away, revealing Becca bursting out of the building, chasing me down, and grabbing me by the shoulders to whirl me around, her face full of apology and regret. As the music soared, we'd cry and laugh and hug as she'd beg me to forgive her. Then we'd sling arms around each other's shoulders and walk off into the snowflakes, a silver-screen-worthy rebeginning of a beautiful friendship.

But my life was not a movie. Becca remained inside with her new friends. And as I walked through the snow-carpeted campus shuffling my boots to make trails in the powder, I remained utterly alone. The wind had started to pick up, and I pulled my parka closer around me, the cold mingling with my despair.

What was going on with Becca? Why was she acting so weird? And how did Olivia fit into all this? Why was Becca hanging around her, obeying her like a pathetic little puppy dog? The Becca I knew would never, ever, in a million years bow down to a Boarder Barbie.

For a moment, as we were crouched down on the floor with the spilled ice cream, I thought I'd caught a glimpse of the old Becca. The Becca who would share chocolate milk with a rumored cootie-stricken outcast. The Becca who would never betray her best friend. Was she still there, somewhere, hiding underneath all the pink ribbons? And if so, how could I draw her out again?

Discouraged, I trudged across campus in the low evening light. The sun was dropping fast, and in a half hour or so it'd be totally dark. As I scanned the empty grounds, my eyes fell upon the half-pipe, a little ways up the hill. I smiled, remembering all the nights Becca and I had snuck out of the dorm, after lights-out, to ride it in the dark. It was the ultimate dare, and we'd never once gotten caught.

On impulse, I changed course, heading over to the ski lockers to grab my board, then starting the short trek up the hill to the top of the pipe. Maybe now was the perfect time to practice—with no one around to see me if I fell. Maybe my only problem earlier had been the pressure of judgmental eyes. Maybe this time I'd be fine and not freak out.

I had to try.

I reached the top of the pipe and looked down. I knew if my life were still that movie, I'd be strapping on my board and dropping in, without a care in the world. The sound track would soar along with me as I popped up over the first side, launching into a perfect back-side 180 tail grab. By the time I'd reached the bottom, I would have successfully not only faced my fears, but completely conquered them. The film would then cut to me at the Olympic games, a gold medal being draped around my neck.

But my life was definitely not a movie, and instead the real-life fear came rushing back like a hurricane wind, practically knocking me over with its force. As I stared down into the pipe, it was as if I could almost see my body sprawled out there, broken and bleeding. My pulse picked up, and my stomach swam. And even though I knew these were all just symptoms of another oncoming panic attack—that they had absolutely no hold on reality—I couldn't manage to let go of either my fear or the horrific images it had chosen to evoke.

And, try as I might, I couldn't bring myself to drop in.

I collapsed onto the snow, no longer able to hold back the tears that had threatened to consume me all day. It was too much. Coming back here to the scene of the crime, dealing with Olivia's sneers, Becca's betrayal, Cam's new girlfriend, my dad's false hope, and worst of all my complete inability to ride down the mountain without falling apart both mentally and physically.

Why had I even come back? There was no reason for me being here. Not when it was crystal clear that my dream had gone down the drain. And without it? I was no one. I had nothing. No hobbies, no sports, no interests, no career goals—my whole life had been consumed by snowboarding up until this point, and if that was really over for good, I had no idea what I was going to do with myself for the next seventy or eighty years.

I was crying so hard I didn't hear anyone approach, until a voice cut through the darkness.

"Are you okay?"

Startled, I looked up with blurry, tear-soaked eyes. A dark, boy-shaped silhouette came into view over the side of the pipe. As he got closer, I saw that he was around my own age. Tall, skinny, with shaggy brown bangs hanging down into his face and a snowboard clutched in his gloved hands. He dropped to his knees in front of me, brushing away his hair and peering at me with concerned blue eyes. He looked weirdly familiar, though for the life of me, I couldn't place him.

"Did you hurt yourself?" he asked, his hands wrapping around my ankles and squeezing lightly. His touch was soft, gentle, and I found myself taking a much-needed breath.

"Thanks, but I'm fine," I assured him, hoping the darkness would hide my tears. I swiped my sleeve across my cheeks just in case.

He gave me a skeptical look, as if he didn't quite

believe me, but pulled his hands away. I guess that wasn't surprising, considering most people who are "fine" aren't found sitting alone, crying their eyes out at the top of a half-pipe. The Boarder Barbies would have a field day if they could see me now.

At least this guy didn't appear to be a Mountain Academy student, as far as I could tell by his ripped jacket and beaten-up board. Most of the kids here were rich as anything or at least sponsored by ski and snowboard companies that provided them with top-of-the-line gear every season. No one at Mountain Academy was stuck wearing duct-taped boots.

"Just a bad night?" he asked, looking me over carefully.

"You could say that."

I waited for him to ask me what happened, wondering what I'd tell him when he did. It was bad enough he caught me crying up here to begin with. What kind of explanation could I give him without sounding like a total loser?

But, to my surprise, he didn't ask. He simply held out his hand. "I'm Logan." He introduced himself. "Logan Conrad."

I stared at him, now realizing exactly why he looked

so familiar. "You're Mrs. Conrad's son," I exclaimed, my embarrassment forgotten. The cafeteria lady always kept photos of her two sons taped to the side of her station.

His eyes dropped to the snow. "Yeah," he replied. "I guess you go to Mountain Academy then, huh?" His voice held a note of disappointment, and I wondered what kind of past run-ins he'd had with my fellow students. Sad to say, staff kids weren't always treated like first-class citizens at my school.

I gave him a sheepish shrug, kind of wishing I didn't have to admit it. "Yeah," I said at last. "At least for now . . . I'm Lexi by the way."

Logan drew in a slow breath. "Well, Lexi, you won't tell anyone at your school I was up here, will you?" His eyes darted around the pipe, as if he half expected ski patrol to pop out from behind a tree and bust him.

I smiled. "Only if you don't tell anyone I was . . . ," I said teasingly.

"Oh. Right." He gave me a shy grin, his shoulders relaxing.

"Don't worry," I said. "My friend and I used to sneak up here all the time at night. We never get caught."

"Yeah, well, I've been caught before. And let me tell

you, it isn't fun," Logan said, picking at a sticker glued to his board. "But it's the only way I can get any time on the slopes. So I have to risk it."

"What do you mean?"

He looked at me sharply. "I mean lift tickets are expensive," he said, his voice sounding a little defensive.

"Oh. Right." My face burned. Of course. Stupid me. Being a full-time student, it was easy to forget that regular people had to pay for every day they spent on the mountain. Like nearly a hundred dollars a day. Not exactly something a cafeteria lady's kid could afford on a regular basis, I guessed.

An awkward silence fell over us. I felt bad, and I knew it was up to me to break it. So I tuned up my best cheesy-TV-announcer voice. The one I used to use to make Becca laugh back in the day.

"So instead you risk your life, sneaking out in the dead of night . . . knowing full well that any second you could be brought down. Tried and convicted of the ultimate crime"—I paused dramatically—"of snowboarding without a license!"

Logan laughed. "That sounds about right."

"Well," I pronounced. "I, personally, think that is

made of awesome. Way to stick it to the man!"

"I'll be happy if I can just stick my jumps, thank you very much."

I giggled. "Don't let me stop you." I nodded toward the pipe. "She's all yours."

"Actually . . . ," Logan said, his voice hesitant again. "I was on my way to a party tonight." He paused, then added, "You don't want to . . . come with me . . . do you? Unless you need to practice . . ."

"Oh, no, no," I said quickly. Probably too quickly. "I'm, um, done here. Definitely done." As if I'd even started.

"Well then do you want to go?"

My pulse kicked up a notch. Did I want to go to a party? The idea was tempting to say the least. To get away from Mountain Academy and spend time with strangers who had no idea who I was—or what had happened.

Still, it was one thing to sneak out here and take a few runs on the pipe after hours. Quite another to leave campus with a strange boy to attend a non-school-sanctioned party. If I got caught, I'd be in huge trouble. With the school itself and, even worse, my dad.

"You don't have to," Logan added, as if sensing my

hesitation. "It's really cool either way. But maybe," he added with a twinkle in his eye, "it might just cheer you up."

I nodded slowly. "Well, in that case," I replied, taking his hand and allowing him to pull me to my feet. "How can I refuse?"

CHAPTER TEN

I followed Logan through the dark woods, lugging my board behind me as the snow crunched under my feet. Where was this party anyway? I'd assumed it'd be back down at the base of the mountain—maybe even in town. But we seemed to be walking straight up the mountain instead. Was the party in the woods somewhere, just off the trail? In an abandoned snowmaking shack? Weren't they worried about ski patrol busting them? It was definitely against the rules for anyone but mountain personnel to be on the slopes after hours.

"Do you have parties up here often?" I asked curiously.

"Sure," he said. "Pretty much every weekend."

"Aren't you afraid of getting caught by snowmakers?"

"Nah. Half the people we hang with *are* snowmakers,"

Logan replied, turning to shoot me a grin. "We've even got some ski patrol friends. Not to mention lift operators, janitors, waiters. Half of Green Mountain's staff either comes to these things or has younger brothers and sisters who do." He shrugged. "Sometimes we can even get one or two of the guys on duty to park their snowcats at the top of the park so we can get some light."

"Wow," I said, surprised and actually pretty impressed. After all, I'd lived half my life at Mountain Academy, and I had no idea that this secret after-hours staff-kid club even existed. And yet evidently we'd shared the same mountain, the same parks, the same trails for years. Me in the daylight, them after dark. It was kind of cool to think about.

"Of course, it's still technically illegal," Logan added. "If the guys got caught, they'd lose their jobs. But the bosses are snug and warm in their beds and there's no one out to bust us."

I nodded thoughtfully. It seemed like the perfect setup.

"Here we are!" Logan announced as we emerged from the woods. My eyes widened in surprise as I realized we were near the top of the Apocalypse itself. The very terrain park where I'd had my big fall earlier today. My stomach knotted a little at the thought of it, but then I reminded myself that no one here would have any clue as to my little misadventure. Or would even care if they did.

The partygoers had stuck small tiki torches along the edges of the park, casting long shadows across the trail. But the dim lighting didn't seem to deter the half dozen or so snowboarders and skiers, hitting the features one by one, or the spectators who cheered them on from the sidelines. Nearby, in the woods, someone had built a small fire, and a few kids were sitting around it, roasting hot dogs and marshmallows over the flames.

I let out a small whistle. "This is pretty awesome," I admitted.

Logan beamed. "Told you," he replied. "I bet you're feeling ten times better already."

"Maybe even eleven," I pronounced, wandering over to the fire and yanking off my gloves to warm my hands. Across from me, a blond-haired guy pulled a guitar from behind a log, while two girls around my age settled at his feet as he started strumming. As Logan joined me by the fire, a few others walked by, waving hello to him and demanding to know why he was so late to the party.

"Fashionably late," he corrected, grabbing a hot dog from a nearby cooler and poking a stick through the center. He held it over the fire. "Unlike you slackers, some of us actually have to work for a living."

Everyone laughed appreciatively, and Logan turned to me. "This is Lexi." He introduced me around. "She'll be slumming it with us tonight." Then he grinned. "Lexi, that's Roland, over there on the guitar. And those are his two bandmates—Scarlet and Lulu."

I waved as the two girls—one with fire-engine red hair and the other with blue streaks woven into a pair of black braids—looked up and smiled. I smiled back, kind of loving the anonymity of it all. Here, I was just Lexi. Not Golden Girl. Not future Olympian. Not "poor girl who got into a horrific accident." Just Lexi. Some random girl of no importance whatsoever.

I was already glad I'd decided to come.

After giving me a welcoming nod, Roland struck up an acoustic version of one of my favorite Lorde songs, and Scarlet and Lulu started singing along in voices that were as loud as they were out of tune. Logan pulled the now-blackened hot dog off the stick and stuck it in a bun, handing it to me with a smile. I took it gratefully, realizing for the first time that I hadn't eaten since lunch—and even then not very much, having lost my appetite watching Becca and Olivia. I took a huge bite. Back in the day, before we'd gotten serious about my career, Dad had taken Mom and me camping in nearby New Hampshire's North Conway area. He was a champion at roasting hot dogs over an open fire. *Just a little burnt,* he'd say. *To help seal in the flavor.* I'd eaten so many I'd gotten sick.

The hot dog Logan made me was just as good, if not better. Or maybe it was simply this place that had everything inside of me finally relaxing for the first time since I'd gotten back. The familiar music. The friendly people. The crisp night air. Everything seemed somehow better here. Simpler. Quieter, even with all the noise.

I kind of never wanted to leave.

"So did you want to take a run?" Logan asked, gesturing to the park. I turned, just in time to watch a skier effortlessly launch over the very jump I'd eaten it on earlier that day. Yeah. No thank you.

"Nah. I'm still winded from the walk up," I replied, using the best excuse I could manage on the fly. "You go ahead though. I'll be fine here." I plopped down onto a nearby log and took another big bite of hot dog, praying he wouldn't press me.

"That's okay," Logan said, surprising me as he sat down next to me on the log. "I'm actually pretty beat from work." He stuck another hot dog on his stick and pushed it into the fire. I gave him a sideways glance. He didn't look tired. Was he just being nice? Or was he actually choosing me over snowboarding? My stomach tingled at the thought. Now that I had chilled out about everything that had happened, I found myself better able to focus on how kind of adorable he was. With his shaggy brown hair and sparkling blue eyes and a jacket that was two sizes too big, he was pretty much the anti–Mountain Academy guy. Which was admittedly part of the appeal.

"So what do you do?" I asked curiously. "I mean, aren't you a little young to have a job?"

He grinned and waved a hand. "A simple technicality," he declared. Then he shrugged. "Actually I just help out my uncle at his gas station," he explained. "Pumping gas, changing oil, patching tires—whatever he needs. It's not the most glamorous of jobs, but he pays me under the table. Gives me cash to enter snowboarding competitions from time to time."

"That's cool," I said. "It must be nice to earn your own money." I'd asked my father last year if I could help him out at the snowboard repair hut, but he'd turned me down flat. Snowboarding *was* my job, he reminded me, and a full-time one, at that. If I ever needed cash, he'd added, I should just ask him. Which sounded like a sweet deal, until you realized all the strings attached to other people's money.

"What about you?" Logan asked. "How long have you gone to Mountain Academy?"

"Since third grade," I admitted, not really wanting to talk about it.

"You must be good then."

"I'm okay I guess."

He stared at me hard, as if trying to place me, and I squirmed under his gaze. The last thing I wanted—I suddenly realized—was for him to recognize me. To realize I was the girl from that terrible accident last year. After all, his mother worked at the school. Of course she would have heard about it.

So when Roland struck up a new song—some grunge tune from the nineties that my mom used to drive my dad crazy with—I leaped from my seat and started singing along with Scarlet, channeling all those nights Mom and I had jammed to her karaoke machine last summer. I didn't normally like singing in front of people—especially strangers—but desperate times and all that.

"Yeah!" Scarlet cried in delight at my unexpected move. "Sing it, sister!"

Soon Lulu joined in, and together we belted out the chorus at the top of our lungs, Logan watching us with obvious amusement from his spot on the log. I knew I was probably blushing hard-core but forced myself to continue singing until the very last verse. Hopefully by then he'd give up on trying to place me.

When the song ended, Scarlet and Lulu shrieked in unison, grabbing me and hugging me with unbridled enthusiasm. Laughing, I hugged them back, my heart still racing in my chest as adrenaline coursed through me.

"That was so awesome," Lulu declared. "Where did you learn to sing like that?"

"Right?" Scarlet agreed, swiping a lock of red hair from her face. "Seriously, Lex, are you, like, in a band or something?"

"'Cause if not, you totally should be!" added Lulu, her eyes shining admiringly.

I chuckled. "Not exactly," I said, trying to imagine fitting band practice into my already crazy schedule. Sadly, the whole Olympic training thing left little room for extracurriculars.

"Do you live here?" Lulu asked. "Do you go to Littleton Junior High? I've never seen you before."

"Lexi goes to Mountain Academy," Logan informed the girls before I could reply. And while he made it sound like a good thing, an important thing even, I caught the girls exchanging knowing looks.

"Oh. That's cool," Lulu replied, with a little too much forced enthusiasm.

"Yeah, you must be super good," added Scarlet encouragingly.

Now I knew I was blushing. It was funny. Before this moment, I'd always felt so proud, telling people where I went to school. As if it made me special somehow. But here it was actually kind of embarrassing.

"I had a friend who once dated a guy who went there. He was, like, always practicing. I'm talking twenty-four-seven." Lulu shook her head pityingly, as if the guy had been stuck in 24-7 detention instead of tearing it up on the mountain every day. "Seriously, he barely ever had time to see her."

"Oh the horror!" Logan broke in, rolling his eyes. "Someone with priorities and a work ethic! Alert the media."

Lulu lobbed a hot dog bun in his direction. "We have priorities, Logan Conrad!" she shot back. "We're going to make Manic Pixie Dream Girl the biggest, baddest band in the whole entire world!"

Logan caught the bun and took a big bite out of it. "Yeah, well, you're going to need a singer who can actually sing, first." He grinned wickedly. "No offense, Rol." The guitar player smirked and kept playing.

"Well, maybe we'll make Lexi our new singer!" cried Scarlet. She flopped an arm around me. "What do you say, Lexi? Want to give up your Olympic dreams for rock stardom? I promise it'll be worth your while. Or, at the very least, warmer!"

She was teasing, of course. But she had no idea how good the prospect sounded to me at that very moment. A free life, without pressure from parents, teachers, and coaches. It sounded like a dream come true.

"Yeah, what do you say, Lex?" added Lulu, shoving Logan out of the way to get on my other side. "Want to be rock stars together?"

"Why not," I declared, leaning against the two of them with as much girl power as I could muster. "At least for the next hour or so."

Whooping loudly, the girls yanked me to my feet and started twirling me around. Roland struck up a fast-paced punk song to match us, and we started dancing madly to the beat, tripping and laughing over one another with bull-in-a-china-shop-style grace. Soon a few others joined in, and suddenly we had an impromptu mountainside dance party going on around the fire. I half wondered, as Scarlet spun me around, how long it would take for someone to fall in and get burned.

For a moment Logan watched us, amusement dancing in his eyes, then his attention turned to something just behind us. I twirled around to see a tall, black-haired guy standing off to the side, his arms crossed over his chest. He looked older, like he was already in high school. He also looked somewhat familiar. Did he work on the mountain somewhere?

"Hunter!" Logan greeted him, rising. "Where've you been all night, bro?"

The guy—Hunter—raised an eyebrow. "In the park, of course," he replied. "Where I assumed you would have been." His eyes fell upon me, critical and cold. "And what do we have here?"

"Lexi, this is Hunter," Logan said, introducing me, and either not noticing the look or refusing to acknowledge it. "He works on the mountain with my older brother, Chris. Hunter, this is my new friend Lexi."

I held out my hand, but Hunter just gave it a dismissive glance, then turned back to Logan. "Can I talk to you?" He paused, then added, "Alone?"

"Uh, sure." Logan said, glancing at me apologetically. "You cool here for a sec?"

"Yeah, I'm fine," I assured him, my heart starting to beat faster in my chest, though I wasn't sure why.

Hunter grabbed Logan by the arm and dragged him a few feet away. They should have been out of hearing range, but mountains had tricky acoustics sometimes, and I could still hear everything he was saying from where I stood.

"What were you thinking, bringing her here?" he

was demanding. "Don't you know she's one of them?"

"Uh, define 'one of them.'"

Hunter leveled his gaze upon my new friend. "Do you even know who she is? Who her *father* is?"

"Darth Vader?" Logan asked hopefully, and it was all I could do not to giggle, even as the unease rose in my throat. Hunter knew who my father was. Which meant he knew who I was. So much for anonymity land.

Hunter groaned. "No, you moron. Bruce Miller," he spit out. "You know, best friends forever with Cy Masters, the guy who owns this place? The one who signs your mom's paycheck every week?"

"So?"

"So everyone in this little shindig is going to get busted once she goes home and blabs about our secret spot to dear old dad." He scowled, then added, "You'll see. Tomorrow this place will be swarming with ski patrol."

"I wouldn't do that," I blurted out, forgetting for a second I wasn't supposed to be hearing any of this. But how dare Hunter accuse me of something like that? He didn't know me. He didn't know anything about me. How dare he try to scare Logan off?

"Sure you wouldn't, sweetheart," Hunter sneered,

glancing over at me. Then he turned back to Logan, cuffing him on the head. "Nice work, dude. Wait till I tell Chris."

And with that, he turned and stormed off back toward the slopes, dragging his snowboard behind him. I watched him go, steam practically coming out of my ears.

Logan approached me, an apologetic look on his face. "Don't listen to him," he chided me. "He can be a real jerk." Then he smiled shyly. "And I'm glad you're here."

"I wouldn't tell my dad," I said again, not sure why I was still arguing the fact.

"I know you wouldn't," Logan assured me. He slung an arm around me, squeezing my shoulder with his hand. It was a friendly gesture, but my stomach warmed inside all the same. "Now come on. I think there's marshmallows around here somewhere. And I make a killer s'more."

There were indeed, and soon we were knee deep in melted marshmallow and chocolate as we watched the riders and skiers take on the park, Roland's guitar sound-tracking the night. Some of the riders were amazingly good, I realized, and a few could probably rival the Mountain Academy teams themselves. Which was pretty incredible, since they were, as Logan informed me, completely self-trained.

"We used to have a ski team at school," he told me. "Sponsored by Green Mountain. But they cut funding two years ago. Along with the free-lift-ticket program for the staff's families." He frowned. "Makes it a lot harder for us to get on the mountain now to do any training."

I opened my mouth to ask why the program had been cut, but a sudden roar cut off my words, followed by blinding white lights streaming through the trees. The party erupted in chaos, everyone leaping to their feet as four snowmobiles approached the scene.

"Ski patrol!" someone screamed.

All around us, partygoers started strapping on their boards and skis and flying down the mountain, abandoning the fire and supplies in an effort to avoid getting caught. Logan looked at me, white-faced, and gestured for me to put on my board.

"Quick!" he cried. "We have to get out of here!"

My heart pounded in my chest as I looked from him to my board, then down the steep hill. This was not good. Not good at all.

Logan paused, in the middle of strapping his board to his feet. "Lexi?" he queried, his voice filled with anxiety.

I swallowed hard. "Go on without me," I told him. "I'll catch up."

To my surprise, Logan started unstrapping his board. "What are you doing?"

'I'm not leaving you."

My heart leaped at his words. "But you have to!"

"Come on, Logan!" Hunter appeared from out of nowhere, board already strapped to his feet. "Chris will kill me if I let you get caught again. Remember what ski patrol said last time."

But Logan just stubbornly shook his head, digging his board into the snow. "I'm staying with Lexi."

"Fine." Hunter rolled his eyes. "Your funeral," he muttered, pushing off down the mountain. But just as he was about to break free, a snowmobile cut him off, forcing him to stop in his tracks.

"Hold it right there," the ski patrol member commanded, climbing off the snowmobile and heading over to Hunter. I held my breath, my heart slamming against my rib cage.

"We're looking for a missing Mountain Academy

student," the ski patrol informed Hunter. "Have you seen a girl named Alexis Miller?"

Hunter turned slowly, his cold eyes leveling on me. My heart dropped to my knees.

"I'm Lexi," I said, stepping forward, toward the ski patrol. At that moment, a fifth snowmobile pulled up behind the others, and the rider yanked off his helmet.

It was Dad.

"Lexi," my dad said in a tight voice. "Get on and let's go."

And so much for rock stardom. Or, you know, even a shred of normalcy.

I turned to Logan, tears in my eyes, and my face full of apology. "I'm so sorry," I whispered. "I had no idea he'd follow me up here."

I waited for the look of regret—or disapproval, to match the one his friend was wearing. Instead, Logan only gave me a small smile. "It's okay," he whispered back. "It was worth it."

My heart pounded in my chest. Suddenly the last thing I wanted was to say good-bye. "How will I find you again?"

"My brother's working the K lift tomorrow," he told

me quietly. "Find him and have him text me." He reached out and squeezed my hand. Quickly, secretly, so my dad couldn't see.

"Come on, Lexi," my father repeated, his voice angry and stiff. I reluctantly stepped down to his snow-mobile, sticking my board into the side compartment, then climbing onto the back. My father saluted the other ski patrol members. "Thanks again," he told them, then looked back at me. "We're going to talk about this when we get home."

He revved the motor, and we pulled away. I looked back, just in time to see the ski patrol members surround Hunter and Logan. Evidently they weren't going to get off so easily.

We drove down the mountain in silence, my father gripping the handlebars. I held on, the wind and snow whipping through my hair. The blizzard was starting to pick up, and in a way I was thankful for a ride home. If only it hadn't come at the expense of Hunter and Logan and the rest of the party. I wondered what they'd do to them. Would they be arrested? Banned from the mountain? I cringed at the thought. Logan could have gotten away. But he stayed. For me. Whatever happened to him would be my fault.

Dad pulled up outside his staff cabin, killed the motor, then dismounted the snowmobile. He turned to me, his face ablaze. "What were you thinking?" he demanded. "Going out to some illegal party with a bunch of staff rats in the middle of a blizzard? Are you insane?"

"They aren't rats," I protested weakly. After all, it was one thing to yell at me—I knew I'd done wrong—but there was no reason to speak badly of Logan! "They were nice! A lot nicer than some of the stupid Mountain Academy students I'm usually forced to hang out with."

"They're breaking the law," my dad pointed out. "Trespassing on mountain property." He raked a hand through his hair. "You just got back, Lexi. You've got a lot of catching up to do. You should be spending your time practicing, not partying, if you want to get back into the game."

I glared at him, my face burning with rage. "Maybe I don't want to get back in the game," I said quietly. "Maybe I'm done with the game altogether."

He looked up, staring at me with horror. "You don't mean that," he protested. "Your dream . . ."

"My dream?" I spit out. "These days it feels a lot more like a nightmare."

CHAPTER ELEVEN

The blizzard raged all through the night, shrouding the campus in blankets of white stuff. Unable to sleep, I lay in my dorm room bed, curled up under my grandmother's homemade quilt, listening to the windows rattle as the storm pounded against them.

I used to love blizzards. Blizzards meant fresh powder and deep snow. They meant rising at the crack of dawn to bribe the lift operator into letting you up on the slopes before anyone else. It was a game, really—a race with the other students to see who could score that coveted first trip down the mountain in a whirlwind of powder. "First tracks" we called them—a one-way ticket down a white wonderland that few tourists would ever get to experience. Once the lifts officially opened, it was too late. The powder got pressed down by the throng or pushed to the sides of the trail. Then it was just another day on the hill.

Until the next snowstorm, anyway.

From the next bed, I could hear Caitlin's soft, rhythmic breathing. She'd been in bed when I'd gotten back, lulled to sleep by the raging storm outside, and it was all I could do not to wake her and tell her what had happened. Of course the person I really wanted to tell was Becca. But I wasn't sure she would be interested in listening. My heart ached as I revisited the scene in the rec center. Her rushing off to do Olivia's bidding. Of course if she hadn't, I might not have met Logan.

I sighed. Logan. The one silver lining in my otherwise lousy first day back. Of course even *that* hadn't ended well, thanks to my dad's misplaced mountainside rescue. I groaned, remembering the look on Hunter's face when he realized that I was the party crasher who had officially crashed the party. I knew I owed both him and Logan an apology big-time. I mean, sure, Logan might have acted more understanding about the whole thing—but I couldn't imagine he had been any more thrilled than Hunter had been to get caught. As he'd told me earlier—he'd been busted before, and it hadn't been fun.

I finally fell into a restless sleep, waking to harsh rays of light streaming through our window. The sun had shooed the storm away, leaving us with pure blue skies and not a hint of wind. I'd slept in late, and Caitlin was already gone—probably off to some extra training session or practice on the pipe. Though we all technically had Saturdays and Sundays off, students who were serious about their careers didn't usually bother with any days of rest.

The question was, was I still serious?

I considered rolling over and snoozing a few more minutes—what else did I have to do that morning? But then I remembered my mission—to apologize to the boys. And the idea of seeing Logan again was nothing if not energizing. Soon I was bouncing out of bed, ready to score the Guinness world record for the shortest shower. After that it was just a matter of layering on the clothes and heading out to the K lift, where Logan's brother worked.

By the time I reached the Green Mountain base lodge, the place was packed with people. Not surprising—the first big dump of the year always got the tourists excited. Snowmakers could have made ten feet of snow earlier in the year, but no one thought of skiing until they woke up to powder in their own backyards. But now that the season had officially begun, weekends would be crowded for the rest of the year.

I pushed my way through the crowd, ignoring the tempting smells of hot chocolate and pure Vermont maple syrup wafting through the air from the Waffle Hut. There would be time for breakfast later. Right now I was a girl on a mission.

I reached the K lift and found a brown-haired guy in a Green Mountain parka working to herd a group of excited grade-school kids into an orderly line. When I told him who I was and who I was looking for, he grinned, and I wondered what Logan had said to him. He told me to wait at one of the picnic tables on the main lodge's deck and he'd let his brother know. Heart thumping, I hurried over to the tables, selecting one near the front so Logan could find me easily. Then I pulled out my e-reader and started reading. After a few minutes I slipped it back in my pocket. There was no way I could concentrate on the story with my mind racing a mile a minute.

"Hey, Lex."

A shadow crossed over me, and I looked up to see a tall figure dressed in a Burton hoodie, with the hood pulled far over his head, obscuring his face. At first I wasn't sure who it was, but then I caught a hint of sparkling blue underneath the hood.

"What, are you in the witness protection program or something?" I teased as Logan sat down across from me at the picnic table.

He laughed and pulled down his hood, a shock of messy brown hair tumbling into his eyes. "Nah, just banned from the mountain for the next two months," he admitted, brushing back his locks. "Thanks to the hardworking efforts of the Green Mountain ski patrol."

I cringed at his words. This was all my fault. Because of me, he'd gotten punished. "I'm sorry," I said with a moan. "If I had known my dad was going to—"

Logan reached out and pressed a finger against my lips, effectively silencing my apology. "Don't worry about it," he told me, sounding sincere and serious. "It's not the first time I've been banned from the mountain. And it certainly won't be my last." He gave me an impish grin. "Besides, I have my superpowers, remember?"

he added, reminding me of my joke the night before.

I smiled in relief. "How could I forget?" After a pause I added, "It was a good party. I mean, besides the end part. Just what I needed. Thanks for taking me."

Logan nodded. "Anytime." Then he shrugged sheepishly. "Well, anytime we have another mountainside party that is. Which, admittedly, might not be for a while."

I groaned, banging my head against the picnic table. "Man, your friends must totally hate me."

"Nah. Most people probably thought it was pretty exciting. They live for near-death escapes like that—makes for a good story the next day." He chuckled. "Anyway, only me and Hunter actually got caught."

I made a face. "And Hunter already hates me."

"Hunter hates everyone," Logan replied, rolling his eyes. "So what are you up to today?" he asked. "Are you taking part in that big tournament over at South Side this afternoon?"

I shook my head, wondering again if I should just tell him the truth. After all, though he was obviously too polite to bring it up, he had to be wondering why I froze at the sight of the ski patrol last night and didn't abandon ship like everyone else. But still, I found I couldn't bring myself to do it. It was too nice to have him think of me as a normal girl. Not as someone to be pitied.

"I'm taking it easy today," I told him. It wasn't technically a lie. "Why? What are you—?"

"Hey, bro, what's up?" interrupted Todd Grossman, fellow Mountain Academy student and top-ranked crosser on the boys' team. If I had earned the title of Golden Girl, Todd certainly could have been crowned Golden Boy. Not that you'd ever know it by talking to him.

Todd hurdled the porch's railing, landing in front of Logan and flashing him an excited grin. I raised my eyebrow. Did they know each other? From the way Logan smiled back at him, I realized they must.

"You ready for today?" Todd asked. "It's going to be completely mad with all that fresh powder." He raised his fist. "Time to bomb the cross like a boss, baby!" He bumped Logan. "Booyeah!"

"Sorry, man," Logan said, waving him off. "I'm out."

"What?" Todd cried. "You can't be serious, bro! The Burton rep is going to be there. He's handing out next year's boards to the winners—they're not even in the stores yet." He gave Logan a look. "And you *know* you need a new board."

Logan shrugged helplessly. "Yeah, well, tell that to Green Mountain's finest."

"Oh man!" Todd groaned loudly. "Do *not* tell me you got yourself banned from the mountain again."

"What can I say? I have a gift."

"Dude! How are you ever going to make it to pro if you keep getting yourself kicked off the mountain?" Todd shook his head. "I guess I should be thanking you though. It's going to be a lot easier to win without you at my heels the whole way down."

"Todd! There you are!"

I glanced behind the snowboarder to see Olivia running up the porch, her cheeks flushed from the cold. Or maybe just too much cherry-colored blush. With her hot pink ski jacket and face plastered with makeup, she looked as if she was about to hit the clubs instead of the slopes.

"Oh, hey, girlie," Todd said, putting out his arm and wrapping it around Olivia. Were they a couple now? Ugh. "You need to tell your old man to stop kicking Logan off the mountain, or I'm going to die of boredom during my next race."

Olivia shot Logan a disdainful look. "If he's banned, then why is he here?"

"I think that's pretty obvious," Todd replied, giving Logan a knowing wink. "After all, what guy wouldn't risk the wrath of Masters for a chance to hang out with the lovely Lexi here." He shot me a grin. "By the way, welcome back, Lex."

"Thanks," I said, unable to help a giggle. He was too much.

Olivia's face turned purple. "That's all well and good," she spit out. "But this porch is for paying customers only." Her eyes drilled into Logan. "No staff rats allowed."

"But evidently mean girls are fully welcomed," Todd shot back playfully, causing Olivia to scowl even harder. He laughed and gave her a kiss on the cheek. "Oh, come on, Cujo. Put away your fangs and buy me that hot chocolate you promised me."

He grabbed her and dragged her down off the porch and toward the Waffle Hut. Before they left, Olivia shot Logan a lethal look, as if to say, *I'll be back—and you'd better not be here when I am.* Bleh. What could a nice guy like Todd see in a girl like her?

"I should go," Logan said. I noticed his ears had turned bright red. He stood up so suddenly he knocked over his chair.

"No!" I cried, panic surging through me. "Don't listen to her. She's only trying to—"

Logan waved me off. "I know. But she's not wrong. I'm not supposed to be here. And if she says anything to her dad, my mom might get in trouble." He gave me a wry smile. "It was nice to see you again though," he said. "I'm sure I'll catch you around."

And with that, he stepped quickly down off the porch and walked past the ski lodge. For a moment I stood stock still, not sure what to do. Should I let him go? I didn't want him to get into any more trouble because of me—I'd already ruined his life enough. But at the same time, if he walked out of my life now, I might never see him again.

And I *really* wanted to see him again.

I spotted him in the parking lot, trudging toward the public bus stop at the other end. He was walking slowly, his steps heavy. It wasn't hard to catch up.

"Logan!" I cried as I approached. "Wait up!"

He stopped, turning back to me, a small smile playing at the corner of his lips. "Yes?" he asked.

"Take me with you."

He raised an eyebrow, and I felt my face flush. Where

had that come from? Did I sound cool? Or desperate?

"You mean, back to town?" he asked, just as the commuter bus pulled up to the parking lot behind him. A few passengers—mountain employees by the looks of them—started unloading. I bit my lower lip.

"If that's where you're going," I managed to bluster.

It was totally against the rules, of course. Underclassmen weren't allowed to leave campus without permission—or adult supervision. Never mind leave with a random boy they'd been expressly forbidden to see. If my dad found out, I'd probably end up grounded until the Olympics themselves.

But what choice did I have? Logan couldn't hang out here. And I couldn't let him go.

"Please?" I said, now pretty sure I was coming off as desperate. But I no longer cared.

The bus driver honked, signaling his departure. It was now or never. Logan stood still for a moment, as if trying to decide. I held my breath. *Please let me come. Please don't leave me behind.*

"Okay," he said at last, grabbing my arm and pulling me toward the bus. "Let's go."

CHAPTER TWELVE

E ven though I'd lived on the Mountain Academy campus for most of my life, I hadn't spent a lot of time in the neighboring town of Littleton, Vermont, just down the hill from the school and ski resort. If we were to go out for groceries or maybe catch a movie, my dad always preferred to head in the opposite direction, toward the vacation town of Paddington, just up the road. Paddington was the kind of town everyone thought of when they pictured traditional New England towns. It had white-steeple churches, cozy bed-and-breakfasts, antique shops, independent bookstores, and even a completely restored covered bridge from the 1900s.

Littleton, on the other hand, was Paddington's poorer

cousin, a postindustrial wasteland that probably should have been put out of its misery once the engines of industry ground to a stop in the mid-1800s, leaving crumbling factories, decaying Victorian mansions, and abandoned storefronts behind.

But somehow Littleton struggled on, and eventually the ancestors of these industrial pioneers found new hope and opportunity when Green Mountain opened its resort. Today most of the town's residents worked either at the mountain itself or for some other tourist-fed side business that had grown up along the access road, their entire livelihoods dependent on each year's snowfalls and the winter warriors with fat wallets who visited.

I rubbed my sleeve against the grimy bus window, trying to get a peek outside. I'd never cared much about Littleton before now, but suddenly I was intensely curious about the town that had produced a boy like Logan. This was where he'd grown up, where he went to school. Where he worked and played and ate and slept. I wanted to know everything about it.

"This is our stop," he announced as the bus pulled up to a nondescript intersection. I followed him out of the vehicle and onto the street.

"So, um, where are we going?" I asked, trying to sound casual even though I was more than a little nervous. I'd never snuck away from school before.

"You'll see."

He led me down the snow-caked sidewalk until we reached a redbrick building with no windows and a flickering neon sign that read BILL'S with the B burned out. Logan chivalrously opened the creaky door, allowing me to step inside first.

My eyes widened as I entered. It was a coffee house—but also an arcade. Not just any arcade, though, but an arcade packed with vintage games popular back in the 1980s—the kind my dad used to play when he was a kid. Pac-Man, Dig Dug, Crystal Castles, even Dragon's Lair. I'd tried a lot of them out on our PlayStation—Dad had bought the arcade games collection, jokingly saying he needed some kind of ego boost after losing to me on Mario Kart for the hundredth time. But I'd never seen any of them in their original big-box packaging. I flashed Logan a grin. How cool was this?

"Lexi!"

I suddenly found myself surrounded and smothered by two familiar faces. Scarlet and Lulu descended upon me, hugging me enthusiastically as they chattered about last night's adventure. As Logan had predicted, the two girls seemed to have no inkling as to my involvement in the whole ski patrol thing, thank goodness.

"And Logan! Poor, poor Logan!" cooed Scarlet, releasing me. "Banned from the mountain, once more with feeling. Whatever will he do now, with all his spare time?"

"Why, he'll start hanging out with us, of course!" Lulu chimed in, tossing a blue-streaked braid over one shoulder. "I mean, sure, at first he'll pretend he's only coming here for the video games and strawberry smoothies. But in time, he'll have to admit the truth. He's become a Manic Pixie superfan and he's helpless to resist us!" She crowed loudly, making a huge flourish with her hands, then bowed low.

Logan rolled his eyes. "Oh yeah. Cause that'll happen."

"Manic Pixie?" I repeated curiously, remembering them talking the night before. "That's the name of your band?"

"Yup. Check it." Scarlet pointed a chipped, neon-green-painted fingernail to the other end of the coffee bar, where, sure enough, there was a drum set, amps, guitars, and other such band-type equipment haphazardly sprawled across a small stage. "Bill's my uncle, and he said we could practice here after my mom got sick of us using her garage," the redhead explained. "As long as we promise not to scare off any customers."

"As if Bill *has* any customers besides us," Lulu added, throwing an affectionate look at the older man behind the coffee bar. I realized he was wearing an eye patch over his left eye and kind of looked like a pirate. "We keep him in business with our chili cheese fry orders alone."

"So it's just the two of you?"

"And my brother Roland, who you met last night," Scarlet added. "I play the drums and Lulu is our bassist. Roland's on guitar—and right now he sings, too. Ever since Carla quit the band." She made a face. "But while Roland is admittedly the most amazing guitar player ever, let's just say he . . ."

"Sounds like a sick cow when he sings?" Logan suggested helpfully.

The girls groaned in unison.

"Seriously, the whole situation totally blows," Lulu

moaned. "There's this big battle of the bands thing at school in a few months. We signed up ages ago. The prize is like a thousand dollars. And maybe even a chance at a recording deal."

"But we won't have a prayer with Roland on the mic."

"Hey, I heard that!" Roland cried, coming out from the men's room. He swiped at his shaggy hair, giving the girls a playful grin, telling them he didn't really mind their complaints. Which made me think he really must be as bad as they claimed.

The two girls looked at one another and then turned to me. "You sure you couldn't come sing for us?" Scarlet asked suddenly. "After all, you were amazing last night. We could really use someone like you."

I stared at her, startled by the offer. When they'd said it last night, I'd assumed they were joking around. But now she'd asked again, and this time she looked serious. I had to admit the idea was pretty tempting. Leave all the stuff I was dealing with up on the mountain and do something completely fun and frivolous for once in my life.

But as alluring as the idea was, I knew there was no way I could say yes. Even in a good year I wouldn't have had enough free time for band practice. And this year was going to be tougher than any I'd had before, if my dad had anything to do with it. (And, of course, he did.) I'd dedicated my life to snowboarding a long time ago, and I knew full well the sacrifices I would have to make.

I realized the two girls, along with Roland, were currently staring at me with hopeful expressions on their faces. I sighed, hating to disappoint them. But what else could I do? It was better to come clean now than get their hopes up for something that could never happen.

"Sorry," I said. "But my training keeps me pretty busy. I don't have a lot of free time." I screwed up my face, imagining what they must think of me. I mean, talk about lame.

"No worries," Lulu said in a forced cheerful voice. "It was a silly idea anyway."

"Yeah, you've got way more important stuff going on. It's cool," added Scarlet. She turned to Roland. "Come on, bro. Let's get back on the set. Break's been over for ten minutes now."

The three of them scrambled up on the platform and grabbed their instruments, gearing up to play. As they launched into their first song, an energetic alternative rock number, Roland belted into the mic, while Lulu hopped around the stage, fingers dancing quickly over her sparkly bass guitar. In the back Scarlet pounded on the drums with perfect precision. They were good. Really good. They would have been great with a real singer. Maybe even record-contract great.

I watched them, unable to move and feeling guilty. This band was important to them, I suddenly realized. As important to them as snowboarding was to me and my friends. This was their dream. Their ticket to fame. And I'd just inadvertently made it sound like a hobby.

I turned to Logan and held up one finger, telling him to wait a minute. Then I took a cautious step up to the stage, my heart pounding in my chest. The music cut short, and the three of them looked down at me with questioning eyes.

"I can't join the band," I told them. "But I'd be honored to join you for just one song."

CHAPTER THIRTEEN

One song turned into three. Then three more. Before I knew it, two hours had passed with me on the mic. Sure, I started out kind of rough. I didn't know the songs, and singing with a live band was a lot more challenging than belting out to a karaoke machine like I always did with Mom. But something compelled me to keep going, and by the end of the session I was sounding pretty good, if I did say so myself. Sure, I was no Adele, but truthfully, most of the band's punk rock songs required more well-tuned screeching than actual singing talent. That and dancing around the stage like a crazy person was something, it turned out, I was naturally awesome at.

When I finally stepped off the stage, swiping the sweat

from my brow, Logan approached, clapping his hands. I couldn't help the wide grin that spread across my face.

"That was amazing!" he declared, giving me a huge hug.

"I'm all sweaty!" I warned, laughing. But he didn't let me go, which made me grin even more.

Scarlet and Lulu bounced off the stage, making it a group hug. "You were awesome!" cried Scarlet. "So, so good!"

"We were *all* awesome," Lulu agreed. "In fact, that was, like, the best session ever. Take that, Carla!" she added loudly, waving her fist.

Breaking from the hug, she headed over to the soundboard. She returned a moment later, a small silver object in her hand. I realized it was a thumb drive. "Here," she said, pressing it into my palm. "I recorded the session. Something to remember us by." Her voice was teasing, but held no hint of sarcasm. I'd won their respect, fair and square. A warm happiness settled in my stomach.

"Thanks," I said, slipping the drive into my pocket. "I can't wait to hear it. And thanks for letting me sing. It was amazing. I only wish . . ." I trailed off, not able to voice what we all already knew.

"Hey, it's all good!" Scarlet assured me, patting me on the shoulder. "And if you want to come back—even for just an afternoon—the door's always open."

"Absolutely," Lulu concurred. "You're like an honorary member of the band now."

I beamed at them. An honorary member of the band. I liked the sound of that.

I said my good-byes and then headed back over to Logan, who was at the bar, paying our coffee tab. As I sidled up beside him, he looked over at me fondly. "You were really great," he reaffirmed. "I hope it was fun."

"It was the best," I declared, finding myself grinning like a loon all over again. "In fact, I couldn't think of a better way to spend my Saturday. Thanks for bringing me here."

"Anytime." He grabbed his change and stuffed it into his pocket. "Do you need to head back now? I don't want to get you in trouble."

I considered this. Truth be told, at that moment I never wanted to go back. Not ever, ever, ever. I wanted to live down here in Littleton and sing and dance and forget there even was a school at the top of the hill to begin with. But, of course, that was impossible. At some point someone would realize I was gone. And then they'd tell my dad. And then . . . Well, I didn't want to think about that.

I glanced at my watch. Still, I was pretty sure I could get away with escaping reality for another couple hours. And I really didn't want to say good-bye to Logan just yet.

"I'm good for now," I told him. "But all that singing has made me super hungry. Is there someplace around here we can go grab some food?"

"Actually," Logan hedged. "I kind of told my mom I'd be home for dinner. It's her one day off this week, and I wanted to keep her company."

"Oh," I said, trying not to sound disappointed. Of course Logan should spend time with his mom. That was really sweet of him, in fact. And I could always meet up with him another time. At some point anyway. When I could next sneak away. . . . "That's cool. I can just grab the bus back and—"

"Do you want to join us?" Logan blurted out. Then his cheeks colored. "I mean, it's kind of lame, I know. But she does make really good sandwiches. And I think she might even be—"

"I'd love to," I cried, perhaps a bit too eagerly. Logan laughed.

"Well all right then," he pronounced. He held out his arm gallantly. "Shall we, madame?"

I took it. "After you, my good sir!"

"Oh my gosh, you guys are so cute you make me sick!" Lulu called from the stage, making an overexaggerated gagging noise. Logan gave her a playful wave as we danced out of the coffee house, still arm in arm. I could feel my face flush as the two girls serenaded us out. They obviously thought we were a couple. But in truth, I had no idea if Logan really liked me or was just being nice.

We trudged through the sooty snow a few blocks over and a few more down. About five minutes later we stopped in front of a light blue, triple-decker apartment building with a chipped-paint exterior and a rusty chain-link fence. Not exactly luxury accommodations and yet I found myself gazing affectionately at each crumbling brick. Run-down or not, this place was part of Logan's life. Which made it as awesome as him.

After Logan unlocked the front door, we headed inside, up three flights of stairs, and into his family's apartment. As I stepped inside, I looked around, curious to see the place he called home. It was small, but at the same time clean and cozy and inviting, the smell of freshly baked bread wafting through the air. The carpet, though threadbare in spots, looked recently vacuumed, and the walls were covered with family photographs. My eyes fell upon a school portrait of Logan as a child, complete with two missing front teeth. It made me smile.

Logan caught me looking at the picture. He groaned. "She insists on keeping all those up," he told me. "It's so embarrassing."

"Aw. I think it's cute," I teased. He shook his head and kicked off his shoes. I followed his lead and accompanied him through the living room.

"Hey, Mom, I'm home!"

I turned the corner into the kitchen just in time to see Mrs. Conrad, wearing an apron adorned with frolicking kittens, reach down to pull a puffy loaf of bread from the oven. She glanced over at her son.

"You're late," she scolded playfully. Then her gaze fell to me. "Though now I see why."

Logan rolled his eyes. "Mom, you've met Lexi, right? From Mountain Academy?"

"Of course!" Mrs. Conrad set the bread down on the

stovetop and pulled off her oven mitts. She walked over and pulled me into a huge, pillowy hug. She was soft and warm and smelled like French bread. "It's so good to see you, sweetie. My son has talked of nothing but you since he got home last night."

"Mom!" Logan hissed. I noticed his ears had gone bright red again. I felt my own face flush as well, while a pleased tickle spun down my spine. Logan had talked about me? He had talked about me to his mother? That had to be a good sign, right? Like a "maybe he likes me" sign?

"You two sit down and relax," his mother instructed, waddling back over to the stove. "I'll bring over the bread and soup in just a minute."

I joined Logan at the small kitchen table as his mother bustled around, preparing our dinner. He gave me an embarrassed smile, and I grinned back at him to let him know it was all okay. The last thing I wanted was for him to think he'd made a mistake bringing me home.

"Here you go!" Mrs. Conrad ladled a huge helping of her famous chicken noodle soup into my bowl, then Logan's, then set a basket of the freshly made bread on the table. I grabbed a slice, buttering it heavily before biting into the crusty goodness. It was probably the best bread I'd ever tasted in my life. And the soup was just as good as the kind she made at school. Maybe even better.

Logan's mom pulled a folding chair up to the table, setting a small green salad at her place. After taking a second slice, I offered her the bread basket, but she shook her head.

"None for me," she said reluctantly. "Doctor says I've got to lose weight."

"And get your blood sugar in check," Logan added, giving the mini Snickers bar she'd half hidden under her napkin a critical look. He turned to me. "My mom seems to think random chocolate bars are cool for people with severe diabetes."

His mom waved him off. "I have one tiny little piece a day," she protested. "What harm could there be in that? A candy a day keeps the doctor away!" She reached for her Snickers. But Logan grabbed it first, ripping it open and popping the whole thing in his mouth.

"For your own good," he told her, his mouth full of chocolate.

His mother sighed, staring dismally down at her plain salad. "Yeah, yeah," she said. "It must be nice to be so young and healthy. To be able to eat anything you want and never gain an ounce." She looked up at me. "I bet you can eat five thousand calories a day with your training schedule."

I blushed. "Something like that." At least when I actually had a training schedule. I set down the half-eaten slice of bread a little guiltily.

"Speaking of snowboarding, have you seen my Logan ride yet?" Mrs. Conrad asked, thankfully changing the subject. "He's the best on the mountain. Better than some of the Mountain Academy kids even." She paused, then added, "No offense."

"Mom," Logan groaned. "Please don't start."

"What? It's true!" Mrs. Conrad rose from her seat, salad apparently forgotten. She grabbed my arm. "Come," she instructed. "I want to show you something."

"Let her eat her soup, Mom."

"It's okay," I assured him, giggling as I allowed his eager mother to drag me through the living room and into a small office at the other end of the apartment. Like the rest of the place it was humbly furnished but meticulously clean. Unlike the rest of the place, the walls were covered with trophies, photos, plaques, and ribbons.

"Wow." I whistled, impressed. "Are these all Logan's?"

Mrs. Conrad nodded, a fiery pride in her watery blue eyes. "He'd have a lot more, too, if we could afford to get him into the competitions. He's such a natural talent. And totally self-taught, too."

I sobered, considering her words. Since our tuition paid for all our entries to the various races, I had never really thought about the fact that the hefty fees could end up deterring some of the potential competition. How many naturally talented snowboarders and skiers like Logan were left out of the running solely because of their parents' bank accounts? While other countries scouted out talented athletes early on, putting them in government-funded programs to train them for the Olympics, in the US you basically needed to have gold to go for the gold.

"That's awesome," I said, picking up a trophy and reading the inscription. First place in the half-pipe in some competition from five years before.

Before she could answer, Logan burst into the room. "Come on, Mom," he groaned. "I promised the poor girl dinner. Not a full-service tour of your Logan Conrad metropolitan museum."

"Okay, okay!" Mrs. Conrad threw up her hands, her face a mask of innocence. "So sorry that I have the nerve to be proud of my youngest son!"

Logan groaned, and I followed him back into the kitchen, trying not to laugh. I knew I liked her for a reason.

As we sat down in our chairs, Logan shook his head in the direction of the office and mouthed the word "sorry." I grinned.

"She's proud of you," I scolded him playfully. "And it looks like for good reason, too. That's a lot of trophies in there."

He snorted. "Yeah, well, half of them are from when I was a kid. Back then everyone went home with a trophy." He paused, then added, "Besides, I'm sure you have a room three times that size with all your winnings."

Now it was my turn to blush. My dad had actually turned my old bedroom in his staff cottage into a Lexi shrine of sorts, and yes, it was kind of overflowing at this point. I'd always been proud of the awards—my dad and I would spend hours going through and dusting and polishing each and every one while we reminisced about which race they'd come from. I sighed. Were those days over forever?

I felt Logan staring at me, and I looked up. His mouth quirked in a shy smile. "I'm glad you're here," he whispered conspiratorially.

"I'm glad to be here," I whispered back, a hot flush crossing my cheeks. And I *was* glad, I realized. In fact, at that moment, there was no place else in the world I would rather have been.

"Logan? Can you come here for a second?"

Logan sighed and scrambled to his feet.

"Coming, Mom," he muttered. Then he mouthed, "Be right back!" to me before heading into the next room.

I stared down at my soup, no longer hungry as butterflies decided to throw an impromptu rave in my stomach. I couldn't believe I was actually here. Having dinner with a boy. A boy who maybe liked me. Like, *liked* me, liked me. Suddenly I was really, really glad I hadn't stayed in Florida this winter.

"Sorry about that!" Logan interrupted my fantasy as he walked back into the room a moment later. His eyes were shining. "But good news!"

"Oh?" I cocked my head in question.

He held up two pieces of paper, a big grin spreading

across his face. "I may be banned from Green Mountain," he announced proudly. "But I think Snow Peak would be happy to take my mom's tickets."

I stared up at him, not understanding. "What do you mean?"

"Turns out, Mom's been holding out on me," he explained, pressing the papers into my hands. I looked down, realizing they were two vouchers, good for lift tickets at neighboring Snow Peak, a small ski resort about twenty minutes north of here. "She had these two tickets stashed in a drawer for the last six months," he explained. "Told me she was saving them for a special occasion. I told her this was it." He snatched them back, looking down at the vouchers as if they were made of gold. "Isn't this great?"

The butterflies stopped short. "You're . . . going riding at Snow Peak?"

"*We* are!" he corrected. "Tomorrow, if you're free."

I stared up at him, a million emotions swirling through me all at once, warring for dominance. He wanted me to go snowboarding tomorrow? With him? What was I going to say?

Logan seemed to sense my hesitation. His smile

145

faltered a bit. "I guess it's not a big deal for you," he amended. "I mean you get to ride at Green Mountain every day. . . ."

The hurt in his voice startled me, and I realized, suddenly, just how valuable those two vouchers were to him and his family. Lift tickets were expensive, he'd told me last night. And yet he wanted to give one to me. Giving up an extra day on the mountain, just so the two of us could spend time together, doing something he assumed we both loved.

"I know Snow Peak isn't that great," he rambled on, his once-smiling face taking on a sheen of anxiety. "But the pipe's not so bad. And there's this amazing secret trail on the back side of the mountain—with the best natural cliff hop I've ever seen. Oh and there's this little abandoned snowmaking hut I found halfway down. Perfect for a picnic lunch . . ."

His words tumbled over one another as he mapped out our day. All the places he wanted to take me. His favorite places—the ones that meant something to him. Watching his anxious eyes as he babbled on, trying to convince me this was a good idea, I realized that even though I should say no—that I should tell him the truth about my accident—I couldn't do it. I couldn't let him down.

So, instead, I found myself nodding yes. Telling him I couldn't wait. That I'd meet him bright and early outside of Mountain Academy's front gate so his mom could drive us over.

As I kept talking, as my mouth kept assuring him I was completely down with the plan, I tried my best to shove the rising doubts and fears to the back of my brain, telling myself I'd deal with them later. Right now reality could wait.

Right now it was enough to see Logan smile.

CHAPTER FOURTEEN

Logan's mother said she didn't like the idea of me taking the bus back to Mountain Academy by myself, so she offered to take me in her car instead. And so after dinner the three of us piled into her 1980s wood-paneled station wagon and began to chug up the steep mountain road. I was half-afraid the old boat wasn't going to make it to the top of the hill, but Mrs. Conrad insisted it was the little engine that could, and sure enough, we eventually pulled up to the old guard shack. Logan's mom flashed her employee ID, and a few minutes later she pulled over and idled at Mountain Academy's front gates.

Logan had insisted I ride shotgun, and, as his mother put the car in park, he leaped from the back, gallantly

opening the door for me and offering me a h
me out of the car. My eyes darted nervously a
out, praying no one was around. If someone s
ting out of a stranger's car, they might ask ~~~~ions.
They might even tell my dad. After last night, the last
thing I needed was to be caught with Logan again.

"So I'll see you tomorrow?" Logan asked, looking as
nervous as I felt. I wanted to tell him to get back in the
car before he got caught again. But at the same time I
didn't want him to leave.

"Can't wait," I said with a smile. "I had fun today."

He grinned back at me. "Me too."

And then, to my surprise, he leaned forward, pressing his lips against my cheek. Before I could even regis-
ter the movement, he darted past me, jumped in the car,
and slammed the door shut behind him.

I placed a hand to my cheek. He'd kissed me. Logan
had kissed me. Okay, it was on the cheek, but still! Seriously, if it wasn't for the fear of breaking my neck on the
ice, I'd probably launch into a full round-off back hand-
spring of joy right about now.

Forcing myself to regain some semblance of composure, I skipped back toward my dorm, feeling lighter and

nappier than I'd felt in weeks. Maybe even the entire year. I was out of breath by the time I reached my dorm, my excitement burning like a fever. I slid the key into the lock, then pushed open the door, bursting into the room.

"Caitlin, you will not believe what I—"

I stopped mid-sentence as I realized my roommate was not alone. My father was sitting on my bed, picking at a sticker I'd stuck on the bedpost the year before. He looked up.

"There you are!" he exclaimed, rising from his seat. "Where have you been? I've been looking all over campus for you this afternoon."

His tone was light, cheery. But I could sense an underlying suspicion. Had Olivia mentioned seeing me with Logan that morning? Had someone noticed me getting on the bus? My mind raced—what could I tell him? Obviously not that I'd been hanging out in Littleton with the boy he'd told me not to see. But at the same time, he wasn't necessarily going to buy the normal hangouts— the library, the ski shop—for all I knew he'd already been looking for me there.

No, there was only one possible answer to this question.

"I just got back from taking a few runs," I lied,

feeling guilt swim in my stomach even as I said the words. The last thing I wanted was to give him false hope about my recovery. But at the same time, it was the easiest thing to say.

Sure enough, his eyes lit up. "That's great, honey!" he exclaimed. He crossed the room in two seconds and threw his arms around me, squeezing me into a huge hug. "I'm so proud of you. Getting right back on that horse—not letting yesterday's little fall get you down. Now that's the Lexi I know and love!"

I hugged him back, ignoring the feeling of Caitlin's questioning eyes burning into my back. There would be time to explain to her later.

"I'm sorry about last night, Dad," I added. "I shouldn't have taken off like that. I didn't mean to worry you."

Dad pulled away from the hug, looking down at me with proud, shining eyes. "I know you didn't," he assured me. "You'd had a rough day. You needed to blow off some steam. I totally get it. We had some ragers of our own back in the day, let me tell you. The stories I could tell . . ." He shook his head. "Now come on. We're going to dinner. I've made reservations at Jacques's. We can celebrate you getting back on the mountain today!"

"Jacques's?" I raised an eyebrow. Jacques's was this big, fancy steakhouse over at the Green Mountain Resort Hotel. It was the kind of restaurant you actually had to get dressed up for or they wouldn't let you in. The kind of restaurant my dad had always made fun of, calling it an overpriced tourist trap. So why did he suddenly have reservations for us to go? Something had to be up.

"What, can't a father take his only daughter out somewhere nice?" he protested.

"I guess so," I said with a shrug, pushing the doubts to the back of my mind. "I'll need a few minutes to shower and change though. Can't wear jeans to Jacques's."

"No rush," he told me. "The reservation is at eight. Just meet me outside the restaurant ten minutes before."

"Okay, sounds good," I agreed. At least that would give me some time to work up an appetite for a second dinner.

"Nice chatting with you, Caitlin," my father added to my roommate. "I hope you do well on that history test Monday." A moment later he was out the door.

I turned to my roommate. "Okay, then. That was weird."

"Um, not half as weird as you telling him you went

snowboarding today," Caitlin replied, giving me a skeptical once-over.

"How do you know I didn't?"

"Well, for one, you don't have helmet head. You also seem to be wearing full makeup. Not to mention a wool coat, instead of your Burton ski jacket. And—"

"Okay, okay, Nancy Drew," I cried, holding up my hands in mock innocence. I plopped myself down onto her bed and grabbed her hands, squeezing them tight. "Do you want to hear what I was really out doing then?" I asked, unable to keep the girlie-girl trill of excitement from my voice.

"Uh, duh."

I paused dramatically. Then, "I met a guy."

"Really?" she exclaimed, her eyes widening into saucers. "Who? Is it that new kid—what's his name? He's pretty cute. Or was it—?"

"He doesn't go to Mountain Academy," I interrupted. "His name is Logan. He's Mrs. Conrad's son. You know, from the cafeteria?" I leaned back, swooning a little as I thought of Logan all over again. "You don't even know, Caitlin. He's so nice. And so cute. I met him last night out at the half-pipe and he took me to this

153

awesome party. . . ." I quickly relayed the short version of the story, ending with my dad and the ski patrol busting us mountainside.

"Dude!" Caitlin cried once I was finished. "You're lucky your dad didn't ground you until Easter."

"I know, right?" I shook my head. "I felt really bad about it. I mean, not about me getting caught—I can deal with Dad. But I hate the fact that Logan got banned from the mountain because of me. Evidently he missed out on this big race because of it too. Anyway, I decided to meet up with him this morning to tell him I was sorry. And we ended up going down to Littleton to hang out."

"You went off campus?" Caitlin gasped.

I shrugged. "It wasn't a huge deal. We went to this coffee house that had an arcade and then to his house." Caitlin's eyes widened again. I laughed. "No, nothing like *that*. His mom was there," I assured her. "It was no big deal. We just had dinner and I got to see all his snowboarding trophies. Oh and before that I got to sing with this band." I reached into my pocket and held up the thumb drive. "They recorded it too. I'll have to play it for you sometime."

Caitlin let out a low whistle. "Wow," she said. "And

to think I've been just sitting here, studying for my history test." She grinned at me. "So are you going to see him again?"

I flopped back onto her bed, staring up at the ceiling. "That's the problem," I admitted. "I sort of promised him I'd go snowboarding with him tomorrow. Over at Snow Peak."

"You promised a cute guy who likes you that you'd hang out with him again?" Caitlin gave me a puzzled look. "How is that a problem? I mean, besides you totally breaking school rules for the third time in one weekend. But it appears you don't seem to care about that."

I rolled my eyes. "It's the snowboarding, duh!" I reminded her. "You might remember the last time I attempted to ride down a mountain? I fell flat on my face and then froze. The rescue team had to take me down by sled."

Caitlin snorted. "Oh please," she scoffed. "That was only because of stupid Olivia. I bet you'll be just fine hanging with Logan. Besides, it's not like he won't let you take it easy, knowing the circumstances."

I gave her a guilty look. "Actually . . ."

"Wait, you didn't tell him?" Caitlin cried, disbelief clear in her voice.

I shook my head.

"Why wouldn't you? I mean, no offense, but it seems like something maybe he should know if you've agreed to go snowboarding with him."

I sighed, pulling myself up and off her bed. "I don't know," I muttered. "I guess I just kind of liked him thinking I was normal. Some random, everyday Mountain Academy student, instead of a poor accident victim."

Caitlin gave me a sympathetic look. "Well," she tried, and I could see her optimism engine working overtime as she chose her words. "Maybe it won't be a big deal. Maybe tomorrow you'll suddenly find your feet again and fly down the mountain, just like you used to."

"Maybe," I replied, trying to match her confident tone. "In fact, maybe this is exactly what I need."

But inside I wasn't so sure.

CHAPTER FIFTEEN

For discerning customers who appreciated a five-star-resort-style experience after a hard day on the slopes, Jacques's Steakhouse was really the only option on the mountain. A linen napkin, celebrity-chef-style restaurant, it was *the* place to see and be seen après-ski.

The interior of the restaurant had been designed to look like an upscale log cabin, with wooden-beamed ceilings and chandeliers fashioned out of elk antlers. The walls were covered with Native American crafts, created, I'd heard, by a local Vermont tribe, and the tables had a rustic, unfinished look, though each probably cost more than my dad's monthly salary. The lighting was dim and atmospheric, with scattered tealight candles offering up a romantic vibe, and soft music from a live harpist in a far corner floated through the air.

In short, Jacques's was exactly the type of place that Mountain Academy's headmaster, Moonbeam, would have avoided like the plague. But his jurisdiction began and ended at the school itself; Green Mountain Resort was entirely Olivia's dad's domain. And nothing was too fancy or too pretentious for Cy Masters. In fact, ever since he first bought the mountain back in the nineties, when Olivia's professional-skier mom had begged her husband for a place to train, he'd been working to class up the place. Jacques's was his crowning achievement.

Even though I'd changed out of my jeans and T-shirt and into a red velvet sleeveless shirt and slim-fitting black pants, I still felt underdressed as I met my dad outside the restaurant and followed the hostess inside. Everywhere I looked I saw designer dresses and European suits. Fancy jewelry and diamond watches. The luxury, in sharp contrast to what I'd witnessed earlier in the day down in Littleton, made me a little sick to my stomach.

As we walked through the restaurant, I spotted Olivia and her father, sitting at a table for four at the very back. Great. I prayed the hostess would change course before we had to pass by them. But instead, to my dismay, she not only led us right to them, but actually pulled out a chair next to Olivia and gestured for me to take a seat.

I glanced over at my dad in horror. He just smiled like the Cheshire cat. "Did I forget to mention?" he asked innocently. "We're joining Cy and Olivia tonight."

I could feel Olivia's glare burning into me as I reluctantly took my seat beside her. Evidently *her* dad had "forgotten" to tell her of the extra dinner guests as well. Typical. The two old frat buddies were constantly trying to push us together, and they weren't above resorting to trickery and lies to do so.

This was going to be a long dinner.

"So what are we having today?" Cy Masters boomed, tucking his napkin into his shirt, as if completely unaware of the tension crackling between the two youngest guests at the table. "I'm thinking the cowboy bone-in rib eye for myself. What about you, Bruce?" he added, setting down his menu and addressing my dad.

"That sounds good to me," Dad proclaimed in his usual cheery voice. He looked across the table at me, trying to meet my eyes. "What about you, honey?"

"I don't know," I muttered, refusing to look at him. I couldn't believe he'd had the nerve to trick me like this. "I'm actually not all that hungry. . . ."

"Nonsense!" Cy declared. "You're an athlete. You can't be skipping meals! What do they teach you in that school anyway?" He scanned the menu. "Why don't you try the surf and turf? Chef Michael has the lobster tails imported from a local fishing outfit in Maine. Completely fresh—why this very morning those suckers were still crawling along the floor of the Atlantic."

My stomach clenched at the thought. I wondered if my father would call me out if I lied and said I was actually a vegetarian. Probably. "Um, sure," I managed to say instead. "That, um, sounds great." Better not to make any waves. Just keep my head down and wait for the pain to be over.

"Good evening. Can I start you off with some sparkling water?"

I jerked at the sound of a familiar voice, looking up to see none other than Hunter himself standing at our table, pen and paper in his hand. Logan's brother's friend was now wearing an ill-fitting red suit jacket and matching pants instead of his snowboarding gear.

Oh no, he was our waiter? And here I thought tonight couldn't get any worse.

As he caught my shocked stare, his eyes narrowed for a split second before he went into describing the specials, all smiles and nods. I thought back to him on the mountainside during the party—his arrogance, his swagger. His dismissive attitude toward the rich kids who went to Mountain Academy. It must have killed him to come to work here every day and be forced to bow down to the very people he despised.

People like me. I slumped in my chair, wishing I were anywhere but here. Hunter already thought I was "one of them," and being caught at dinner with the resort's owner and his spoiled daughter was not exactly going to prove him wrong. I wondered if he'd believe me if I got up and told him I'd accidentally sat down at the wrong table. Or, you know, ran screaming from the restaurant altogether. Would he tell Logan he saw me here? Would Logan think less of me if he did?

"And what would *madam* be having this evening?" Hunter asked, turning to me after taking my dad's order. I could hear the sarcastic undertone in his question, so slight the others would probably miss it. I just knew the second he got back to the kitchen he'd be texting Logan and telling him everything. After he spit in my food that was.

"Um, I'll have the—" I stared down at the menu, my face burning, my mind going blank. "The . . ."

"She'll have the surf and turf," Olivia suddenly interrupted. "And please tell Michael not to skimp on the lobster tails this time. That may be fine for tourists, but my invited guests should receive what they're entitled to." She made a humph sound of emphasis, and I wondered how much willpower it took for Hunter not to reach out and strangle her with his bare hands.

But "of course" was all he said, the perfect model of restraint as he scribbled in his little pad. Only his white knuckles gripping his pen gave anything away. No wonder he was such a jerk when he first met me. He was used to people like me being jerks to him first. It was all I could do not to grab him and tell him that I wasn't like that. That I wasn't "one of them." But I knew it would do no good.

"You know," Olivia said, turning to her dad as if Hunter wasn't standing there, right in front of her. "In this terrible economy, you'd think people would be grateful to even *have* jobs. Why, if it wasn't for us, they'd probably be living on the streets." She turned and leveled her eyes on Hunter, as if he was dog doo-doo she'd discovered on the bottom of her designer heels.

"That might be preferable to having to deal with you," I retorted.

Olivia whirled her head around. "What did you just say?"

I opened my mouth to repeat myself, only to have my dad shoot me a warning look. "Lexi . . ."

"Nothing," I said sweetly. "I just wanted to add a side of asparagus to my order."

I glanced over at Hunter. Was that a hint of a smile ghosting his lips? Catching my eye, he gave me the slightest nod of his head—so quick I almost missed it—before moving on to take the rest of the orders. I sat back in my chair, feeling somewhat vindicated.

As Hunter left, Cy turned to my dad. "Now," he proclaimed. "Let's get this out of the way so we can enjoy our dinners." He turned to his daughter. "Olivia? Don't you have something to say to Lexi here?"

Olivia scowled, pursing her lips together so tightly they turned white. Finally she spoke. "I'm sorry," she mumbled, sounding anything but.

"What was that?" her father demanded. "I don't think anyone heard you."

"I'm sorry!" she spit out, this time with overexaggerated volume. "I'm sorry for making fun of you when you fell yesterday. I know you had a serious injury and it'll take some time to get back to where you were. If you need any help along the way, please let me know and I'll be happy to aid you in any way I can."

She spoke the words in a monotone and a little too fast, as if reciting from a script. One penned by her dear old dad, I was sure. I sighed. I knew the two parental units meant well, but couldn't they see this kind of thing only made everything worse?

"That was very nice, Olivia," my dad remarked in an oh-so-patronizing voice that only served to make Olivia wrinkle her nose in annoyance. Then he turned to me. "Well, Lexi?" he asked, raising an eyebrow. "Is there something you would like to say to Olivia?"

I had many things to say to Olivia. Like, hadn't she already done enough, sabotaging me on the slopes, then stealing away my best friend? Did she really feel the need to keep on ruining my life for the foreseeable future?

But instead I said only, "I'm sorry for shoving ice cream in your face."

Cy Masters burst out laughing. Olivia looked as if she'd swallowed worms. "Sorry," Cy said quickly, regaining his composure. "I hadn't heard that part." He shook his head. "I gotta hand it to you, Bruce. Your daughter is a spitfire. Just like her old man. You better watch out, Liv. With spirit like that, she's going to be back on the mountain in no time flat—kicking your butt in every race—just like her old man used to do to me!"

I cringed. I knew he just meant to be funny—but for Olivia this was anything but. "Look," I tried. "Olivia's actually quite—"

But she was already gone, up from her chair, coat in hand, before stampeding toward the restaurant's exit like a wild horse. The other diners stopped their conversations and watched her go, curiosity, rather than sympathy, sparking in their eyes.

Cy turned to my father. "What did I say?" he asked, completely clueless.

I rose from my seat, forcing my movements to be slow and calm, even though all I wanted to do was scream.

"Excuse me," I said. "I . . . don't feel well."

Now the stares turned to me as I headed out of the restaurant, but I ignored them all, pushing past the lengthy line of people waiting to get in and down the hall toward the exit. As I turned the corner, I almost tripped over Olivia, who had crouched down against the wall outside the ladies' room, hugging her knees, her face buried in her arms. I could hear the muffled sobs coming from below.

I knew I should walk on, leave her to her well-deserved misery. And yet somehow I felt an unwanted stirring of pity deep inside—some strange fellowship over our two totally meddling fathers—and found myself sliding down the wall to sit beside her.

"You okay?"

She looked up, her face blotchy. "Go away."

"Look, I'm sorry about all that," I said awkwardly, not sure the best way to comfort her. Or if I should be comforting her at all. "I'm sure your dad was just joking. He didn't mean it."

"Of course he meant it," Olivia snapped back, her voice filled with venom. "Do you think that's the first time he's said something like that to me?"

I shook my head slowly, remembering the scene

outside the rec center. Where, once again, her father had used me as a means to cut her down. No wonder she hated me so much. I'd kind of hate me too.

"Nothing I ever do is good enough for him," Olivia went on, staring at the wall across from her. "If I get an A, he'll want to know why I didn't get an A plus. If I win a race, he'll say I just got lucky." She squeezed her hands into fists. "I so wish Mom was still alive," she uttered, more to herself than me. "It was so much better then."

My heart ached at the raw pain I heard in her voice. It was hard to remember, when suffering through her daily dose of meanness, what she'd had to go through two years before when her mom lost a long battle with breast cancer. The two of them had been so close—best friends in a way. She must miss her like crazy. And while, sure, that didn't excuse all the nastiness and arrogance and certainly not the sabotage on the slopes, it did help me remember that she wasn't a total monster deep down. Just a girl who missed her mom.

"I'm so sorry," I murmured, daring to lay a hand on her arm. "I can't even imagine what that must be like."

For a moment Olivia let me put my hand on her. Then her face twisted, and she jerked her arm away. As if she suddenly realized exactly who she was allowing to comfort her.

"What do you think you're doing?" she growled.

I stumbled backward, a little shocked. I wanted desperately to tell her it was okay—that I wouldn't tell anyone I'd caught her in a moment of weakness. But I knew it would do no good. She'd just inadvertently shown her soft underbelly to her worst enemy for the second time in a week, and I was going to have to pay for what I saw.

"Look, Olivia," I tried, holding out my hand. "It's no big deal. I'll help you up and we'll go—"

"Get away from me!" she screeched, her voice choking on the words, which only served to make her angrier. "Don't even pretend like you care!" She turned toward me. My eyes widened. Was she actually going to hit me? I could feel the eyes of those waiting for a table on us, as if we were part of some kind of reality TV show. What would I do if she hit me? I couldn't hit back—I'd get expelled from school! But I'd have to defend myself somehow. . . .

"Olivia, stop!"

A familiar voice broke through the noise. I looked up to see Becca pulling Olivia to her feet. What was she doing here? Had Olivia texted her or something? Asking *my* best friend to come to *her* aid? I could hear Olivia protesting over Becca's soft but forceful words.

"Calm down." Becca was soothing my enemy. "She's not worth it."

I sat there, stunned, as I watched her take Olivia by the arm, leading her out of the restaurant and into the night, her words still echoing in my ears. Words Becca had said to me a thousand times before—in other fights involving Olivia.

But today it was me who was "not worth it" in my best friend's eyes.

CHAPTER SIXTEEN

woke up the next morning to a perfect ski day. The kind of day I used to live for, back when I was regularly competing. The sun shone; the wind was nonexistent. And the temperature was crisp, but not bitter cold. Enough to keep the ice away, without having the hill devolve into slush.

As I pulled my snowboard pants over my black leggings, I felt an unfamiliar excitement start to build. A feeling of anticipation swirling up inside of me. I honestly thought I'd feel more anxious, given what I was about to undertake. But the knowledge that I was going to spend the day with Logan gave me a warm glow that even reality couldn't take away.

"Where are you going?" Caitlin asked sleepily,

peeking out from under her black bedspread. "It's early—even for you."

"I'm meeting Logan," I reminded her. "We're going to Snow Peak today."

Caitlin shot up in bed, sleep forgotten, her eyes dancing with excitement. "Oh, yeah!" she cried. "Are you nervous?"

"I'm terrified!" I said with a laugh. "But excited, too. I can't wait to see him."

"Aw," Caitlin cooed. "It'll be so romantic. Just the two of you, all alone on the slopes . . ."

"With about a thousand other people."

"But you won't notice a single one of them," Caitlin pronounced, refusing to be deterred. She rolled over, propping her head up with her elbow. "Do you think he'll kiss you?"

"Argh!" I cried, throwing a pillow at her. "Stop it! You're killing me here!"

Caitlin grabbed the pillow and hugged it to her chest. "You'd better tell me every detail when you get back. Every single awesome detail."

Speaking of details . . . As I pulled my sweater over my head, I wondered if I should tell Caitlin what

171

happened last night with Olivia, but then decided against it. Though Caitlin was a good person, she was also, well, very . . . friendly. And not the best at keeping secrets. I was pretty sure that if I told her now, half the school would end up finding out by lunchtime. Which would only serve to further enrage you know who all over again. And funny enough, I had no desire to keep sticking my hand in that particular hornet's nest, thank you very much.

Man, I missed Becca. Becca was my rock. My Fort Knox of secrets. I could—and would—tell her anything and everything. I missed that.

I missed her.

After stuffing my feet into my boots and saying good-bye to my roommate, I headed downstairs, grabbed my snowboard out of my locker, then changed course to meet Logan and his mother at the front gate. As I crossed under the archway, I found myself glancing up at the inscription again, whispering the words under my breath.

"'What would you attempt to do if you knew you could not fail?'"

I'd come up with a thousand choices over the years

as I'd walked under that archway. Most of them having to do with sacrificing everything to go for the gold. But today a different choice made its way through my mind. I would choose, I decided, to spend one grand and glorious day on the slopes with the most interesting boy I'd ever met. And not waste one single moment of that grand and glorious day being afraid. It wasn't an Olympic-size goal, to be sure. But at the moment it felt nearly as important.

As I approached the circular driveway, my heart skipped a beat as my eyes fell upon Logan's mother's station wagon. Logan hopped out of the front passenger seat and cheerfully opened the back hatch of the car. He took my snowboard from me and loaded it up, then joined me in the backseat.

"Are you ready for the best day ever?" he asked, his eyes gleaming with excitement as his mother put the car into gear and started down the Mountain Academy driveway. "I could barely sleep last night I was so psyched."

I giggled, trying to tell myself that he was just excited about snowboarding itself—after all, he didn't always have an opportunity to score a free lift ticket. But something deep inside of me wondered if perhaps even a tiny part of his insomnia had something to do with seeing me again. I hoped so anyway.

We arrived at the mountain about twenty minutes later, with Logan's mom pulling up to the drop-off spot and handing Logan the vouchers. "You have fun," she instructed. "I'll be back to pick you up around three when I get off of work."

"Thanks, Mom," Logan replied, grabbing the vouchers and leaning over into the front seat to kiss his mom on the cheek. I smiled to myself; it was so sweet to see how well he treated his mother.

We scrambled out of the car, slamming the doors shut behind us. After we grabbed our boards and bags from the back, his mother pulled away, leaving us alone together. I bit down on my lower lip as the reality of what I was about to attempt reared its ugly head. Logan was going to expect a professional, well-trained snowboarder. What was he going to think of me if I couldn't perform to his expectations? Which admittedly was an all-too-likely scenario, based on what had happened on Friday.

"So what trail do you want to hit first?" Logan asked after we dumped our bags in the lodge, traded our vouchers for tickets, and headed outside to the chairlift. I knew he was trying to be patient, but he was also super excited to take that first run. His enthusiasm made him even more adorable in my eyes. But it did nothing to stop my nerves.

He scanned the map, then handed it to me. "Unfortunately there's nothing as crazy as over at Green Mountain," he added, sounding apologetic. "In fact, the whole place is really just a big hill. But, you know, beggars can't be choosers." He flashed me a grin as he handed me my lift ticket.

I took it, turning it over in my hands. "It's perfect," I assured him. After all, the last thing I wanted right now was a challenging double-black-diamond trail. And the fact that none of my snobby classmates would be caught dead on "Slow and Weak," as they'd dubbed Snow Peak, was a dream come true. In fact, this was pretty much the best possible place to find my feet again, and I was determined to make the most of it. Especially since Logan had given me a free ticket. I'd tried to tell him I'd pay for my own—not wanting him to waste the precious voucher on me—but he insisted on it being his treat. I'd only have insulted him by refusing it.

We headed over to the antiquated two-person chair-lift, slow as molasses compared to the high-speed quads over at Green Mountain. We got in line, watching the chairs groan and creak as they cranked up the mountain-side. Once upon a time Snow Peak Resort had been a thriving slice of Vermont's ski and snowboard culture, but when the economy was hit hard, smaller resorts like this one struggled to survive. It was too bad, really. Snow Peak was a great mountain for families. And I kind of liked the nonpretentious vibe. No one here worried about showing off top-of-the-line equipment or dressing to impress in ridiculous designer outfits. They came only to snowboard or ski. And to hopefully have fun.

We rode the chair to the top and dismounted, with me somehow managing not to fall on my face this time. Logan pointed to a nearby trail, and I followed him over to it, dragging my board behind me. As I approached the drop-off, my eyes fell upon the trail marker. Ugh. A black diamond. I tried to tell myself that a Snow Peak black diamond was probably only as difficult as a Mountain Academy blue square—a medium-difficulty-level trail—but it didn't stop my pulse from kicking up to an anxious beat.

As if in response to my sudden anxiety, my board hit a chunk of ice, causing me to stumble. Logan grabbed me before I could fall. "Steady now," he teased, his eyes sparkling. "Don't want you to hurt yourself before you even get started!"

I laughed, but it sounded hollow. I knew he was just being funny, but I didn't need the reminder of the possibility of getting hurt. As I sank to the ground, to strap in my right foot, I forced myself to take a peek down the trail. I swallowed hard at what I saw. Everyone always ragged on Snow Peak as being too easy, but from my vantage point, it looked like a steep cliff, dropping off into a snowy abyss. My heart started slamming against my chest, and my pulse began to race. I tried to do the breathing exercises the nurse had taught me on Friday to calm my nerves, but they didn't seem to be working.

"You ready?" Logan asked, as he hopped to his feet and bounced on his board. He offered me a hand, and I took it with shaky gloved fingers, trying to find some sort of strength through his grip as I pulled myself to my feet. But instead, my knees wobbled, and my legs threatened to give out from under me.

What had I been thinking? Did I really believe I'd

just be able to forget all that had happened and become my old self again, simply because I was with a cute boy? Why, this was even stupider than what I'd pulled on Friday, going down the terrain park to prove myself to a bully. And if it ended the same way, which, let's face it, was a definite possibility, then what would Logan think of me? To him, I was this cool snowboarding chick, a hot rider from an elite school. He was expecting a killer day on the slopes—with me not only keeping up, but probably surpassing him in skill. After all, I'd been given all the advantages he'd been denied. What was he going to think when I fell flat on my face?

I should have told him. I should have spoken up before we cashed in those vouchers. Because now it was too late. I had let him waste those precious free tickets on someone who wasn't even going to be able to do one single run. He could have invited someone else. Or gone alone twice. But no. I'd kept silent, ignoring reality, hoping for a miracle, and now he was the one who was going to pay for my patheticness. It'd be a wonder if he ever talked to me again after what I was about to have to admit.

"See you at the bottom!" Logan cried, completely

oblivious to my inner nervous breakdown. He gave me a wave then dropped in, effortlessly gliding down the trail and leaving me behind.

I willed myself to push off. To at least attempt a single run. *No one's watching. It's no big deal,* I tried to tell myself. But as I stared down the precipice, begging my body to obey my mind, the landscape loomed and spun, throwing my already topsy-turvy stomach into a tailspin. My heart continued to pound, and my fingers went numb.

I couldn't do it. I just couldn't convince myself to let go.

I plopped down on the snow, my head in my hands, embarrassed beyond belief. Logan was going to regret the day he ever met me, I was sure of it.

"Lexi?" Speak of the devil. Logan called up from about fifty yards down. He'd stopped to wait for me, I realized. Which was really sweet. But he'd be waiting a long time. "Are you okay?"

I couldn't even bring myself to form an answer. Because, really, what could I say? That I *was* okay—but I was just going to hang out here all day instead of taking a run? Or that I *wasn't* okay? That I'd conveniently forgotten to tell him I could no longer snowboard? Neither answer seemed like a good idea, so I just waved him on, yelling that he should keep going and I would "catch up later." Whatever that meant.

But I had underestimated Logan. And a few minutes later he was by my side again, having unstrapped his board and hiked back up the side of the trail.

"What's wrong?" he asked, giving me a worried once-over. "Did you hurt yourself?"

I wanted to say no. But instead the "yes" burst from my lips, and I found I was unable to hide the truth from him a moment longer. The words tumbled over one another as I told him all about the accident, my therapy, Friday on the slopes when a panic attack had derailed me. The panic attack that had now resurfaced as I stared down the hill.

"I'm so sorry!" I sobbed, the tears pouring from my eyes as I finished my confession. "I wanted so badly to spend the day with you. I thought I could do it. I really did. But I can't. I just can't. And now I've gone and wasted your mom's lift ticket and—"

"Hey, hey!" Logan cried, grabbing me and pulling me into a huge bear hug. "It's okay, Lexi," he assured me. "It's really okay."

"But you could have given the ticket to someone else," I choked out. "You could have come here twice yourself. Instead of completely wasting it on me."

"Oh, Lexi." He released me from the hug to find my eyes with his own. As I dared myself to meet his gaze, I searched for anger, disappointment, annoyance—even pity—but found none of the above. Only concern and compassion shone in his eyes.

"I don't care about snowboarding," he told me. "I wanted you to have fun. That's all. Whether it's out on the slopes or sitting in a lodge—it's all good to me."

"But—but—" I stammered. I wanted so badly to believe him. But still. "I'm sorry," I said at last. "I feel so stupid. I guess I just wanted you to think I was normal."

To my surprise, he chuckled. "Please. In my experience normal is completely overrated." He reached out and unstrapped my board from my boots. "Now come on," he said once he was finished. "We'll take the chairlift down. Have you ever done that? It's actually pretty cool." He grinned. "And then we'll order large hot chocolates with extra, extra whipped cream. And I know an awesome spot by the fireplace. We can hang out and play games and talk and . . ." He shrugged impishly. "I think it sounds like the best day ever. What about you?"

I stared at him, scarcely able to believe my ears. He'd willingly give up an entire day of doing something he loved more than anything—something he didn't often get a chance to do—just to spend time with me? It seemed unbelievable. Until, I realized, I would have done the exact same thing for him, had the tables been turned.

"Come on," he said. "I'll race you to the lift."

He was right; despite the amused looks of the lift operators, it was pretty cool to go down the chairlift. The pressure seemed to drop with the altitude, and by the time we reached the bottom of the hill, I was feeling pretty good about things. Good enough, in fact, to suggest that we go hit the bunny slope instead of going inside.

And so we did.

I'm not going to lie; the first trip down the beginner's trail had my heart racing all over again, and I wasn't halfway down before I tripped on an edge and fell flat on my face. But before I could manage to wallow in humiliation city, Logan was by my side, his hand outstretched and his face full of encouragement. I found myself grabbing his hand gratefully and pulling myself back to my feet, continuing down the mountain. It was a slow and torturous journey, but eventually we found ourselves at the bottom of the hill.

"Whoo-hoo!" Logan cried, whooping loudly and offering up his hand in a high five. "You did it!"

"A four-year-old could have done it," I muttered, forcing myself not to leave him hanging, even as my cheeks burned. "Most likely without falling on her butt five times on the way down."

"Who cares?" Logan scolded. "Everyone falls. It's no big deal. Seriously, Lex, you need to lighten up."

"I know but . . ." My face twisted. "You don't understand. If I don't get back to where I was . . ."

"Forget that. Forget all of that," he insisted, his blue eyes focused on me. "At least for today. Just forget about your training, the Olympics. All of it. Pretend you're only out here to have fun. You do know how to snowboard just for fun, right?"

Did I? I'd been training so long. So hard. The idea of snowboarding just for fun—without worrying about speed or form or skill—it seemed like a foreign concept.

But Logan wasn't about to take no for an answer. He reached down, scooping up a large handful of sticky snow, his eyes shining mischievously. "Do I need to teach you the meaning of fun, young lady?" he teased, stepping toward me, snowball raised and ready.

I shrieked and scrambled out of the way, grabbing my own fistful of snow and readying my aim. "Don't you even think about it!" I cried. "I've got a killer arm and I am not afraid to use it."

"Yeah? Well, you'll have to catch me first!" he cried, kicking off on his board with his back foot and gliding toward the magic-carpet lift that led to the top of the bunny slope. Giggling, I planted my own foot on my board, following his lead. A moment later we were both headed back up the hill, panting and laughing.

And totally ready to have fun.

CHAPTER SEVENTEEN

The day ended far too soon, and before I knew it we were back in the lodge, in front of the fire, peeling off layers of jackets, hoodies, ski pants, and boots, preparing to meet Logan's mother outside. We were still laughing, and my cheeks were flushed from a mixture of wind and excitement. Even though we'd never gotten farther than a green-circle easy trail, I couldn't remember the last time I'd had such a good time on the slopes. Logan had been right; over the past year I'd been so concerned with the competitive aspects of the sport that I'd forgotten how much I just loved the feeling of the wind against my cheeks and the snow under my feet.

But all good things must come to an end. We

reluctantly piled into Logan's mother's station wagon and started back to Mountain Academy. The trip was at least a half hour, but it felt like only a few precious minutes before we were pulling up to the guard shack outside the school.

I watched as Logan pulled out my gear from the back of his mom's car, setting it down on the sidewalk. "When can we do this again?" I blurted out, unable to stop myself. The day had been a dream come true, but now we were back to real life. Tomorrow I had classes and my training sessions, and Logan had public school and probably work at his uncle's garage. Even if he did manage to get an evening off, he was still banned from the mountain and couldn't come for a visit.

Then there was my dad, who thought Logan was bad news. A lowly staff rat, unworthy of his ice princess. How could I make him see that Logan was the exact opposite? That a thousand training sessions with the coach he'd hired wouldn't be half as effective as a single day on the mountain with Logan by my side?

"Hey!" Logan exclaimed, catching my face. He grabbed me and pulled me into a hug. "We'll make plans for the weekend, okay? I'll make sure I get Saturday off work. Maybe we can go to a movie or something. How about that?"

"That'd be cool," I said, trying my best to sound casual, though inside I was dancing with excitement. A week was a long time, but we could always text and stuff. Maybe even play some online video games.

"In the meantime," he added, "you have to promise me you'll keep practicing. And that once in a while you'll just go out and snowboard for no reason at all— except to have fun."

"I think I can handle that," I said with a grin.

"Good," he declared. Then he wagged his finger at me. "And anytime you start feeling the pressure—from your coach or your dad or whatever—you just remember that I think you're awesome. And who are *they* to tell me *I'm* wrong?"

I laughed out loud. I couldn't help it. Suddenly I found myself wanting to hit the biggest jump I could find in the park—at full speed for the whole world to see. And I could do it too. Because Logan thought I was awesome.

And if Logan thought I was awesome, well, who cared about anyone else?

CHAPTER EIGHTEEN

Ten minutes later I was opening my dorm room door. Caitlin wasn't there, so I dumped my bag on my side of the room and decided to put on some music to help me wind down. After scrolling through my iTunes collection for a few minutes, trying to decide what to put on, I remembered the Manic Pixie Dream Girl recording Scarlet had given me before I left Bill's yesterday. I slipped the thumb drive into my MacBook, my finger hovering over the play button. I was admittedly more than a little nervous to hear it—to discover whether I really was any good or if they were only being polite. Then I remembered Logan's parting words. He thought I was awesome.

I hit play.

The first song burst through the speakers, Roland wailing on his guitar, Scarlet pounding out the beat. I lay back on my bed, staring up at my ceiling, wringing my hands together nervously as the vocals kicked in. At first my voice sounded tinny and small—and I could hear the uncertainty as I stumbled over the unfamiliar lyrics and tune. But by the third or fourth song I seemed to have found my groove, and a rich, powerful voice started belting out from my computer speakers, actually giving me goose bumps. Was that really me? I had to double-check the thumb drive to be sure. I sounded good. Really good. Guess all those misspent nights with Mom doing karaoke had really paid off.

"Hey, is that Manic Pixie Dream Girl?" Coach Basil poked her head into my room. "I recognize the song, but they sound different."

"You know Manic Pixie?" I asked, sitting up in bed, surprised. I knew Coach Basil was a huge indie-music fan, but still!

"Sure," my coach replied, entering the room and plopping down on Caitlin's bed. She nodded her head in time to the beat and mouthed a few of the lyrics. "One of the girls' moms works in the admin building here at

Mountain Academy. She heard I liked music and gave me one of their demos—to see what I thought of it." She paused, then added, "She told me the other day they were all bummed out 'cause their singer quit on them. Sounds to me like they found a pretty good replacement."

Wow. I hugged my knees to my chest, feeling my face flush. Should I tell her? "Um, that isn't their replacement," I confessed, deciding to go for it. "That's just me."

Coach Basil cocked her head in confusion. "What do you mean, just you?"

I stared down at my lap. Maybe I shouldn't have said anything. "Just me, singing?" I finally explained. "I met up with them yesterday and we messed around a little. No big deal." I swallowed hard as I realized I'd just basically admitted to going off campus without permission. Hopefully, she wouldn't pick up on that.

"Are you kidding?" she cried, luckily in music-lover versus den-mother mode. "It's huge! Lexi, you sound incredible. I mean, I've overheard you singing in the shower a few times, but this!" My coach paused, listening intently as the second song ended and the third began. "Were you auditioning for them?" she asked. "Are you looking to join the band?"

"Well, they did ask me," I admitted. "But, of course, I can't do it. I mean, there's no way with all my training and school and stuff. I lost a whole year because of the accident; I have to work double-time to catch up. Maybe even triple. Which doesn't leave me any time left for things like band practice."

Coach Basil's enthusiasm deflated a little, and I got the weird feeling that I'd somehow let her down. "I suppose you're right," she said at last. "The schedule they keep you girls on . . ." She shook her head. "I remember what it was like. All that dedication. No time for anything else. And then . . ." She trailed off, staring into the distance.

I knew exactly what she was thinking about. Her own stalled-out career after an accident like mine prevented her from competing. It was all-too-familiar territory for me now.

"How . . . ?" I started, not sure how to phrase my question. Coach Basil turned to look at me sharply. "How did you know?" I finally managed to say.

"That my career was over?" she asked pointedly.

I grimaced, but nodded, both wanting and not wanting to know the answer at the same time.

191

"I didn't at first," she confessed. "I kept trying to get back to where I was before the accident. I trained every free second. I signed up for every race. I didn't let myself take the time to allow my body to properly heal. And so, a couple months later, I injured myself all over again." She frowned. "I was lucky I didn't paralyze myself that time. Doctors said if I had fallen one inch differently, I would never have walked again, never mind snowboarded." She paused. "After that, I had to face the truth."

"That your dreams were over forever," I concluded with a long sigh. Everything she'd put into the sport, everything she'd sacrificed to become the best—it had all been for nothing. Would that be my fate as well?

Her eyes turned stern. "Okay, so I can tell you're totally missing my point here," she said. "All I'm trying to say is I pushed myself too hard, too fast. I was so worried about being forced to give up my dream that I made it happen all by myself."

I hung my head, hearing all too well what she wasn't saying. She had been too worried about me, after my fall, to properly scold me for going against her orders. But now I was in for it.

"Look, Lexi," she continued, giving me a sympathetic look. "I know how much you want to prove to everyone that you're fine. I was the same way back then. But pulling stupid stunts like you did in my class on Friday—well, that's only going to prove the opposite. And it could get you hurt—all over again."

She was right. Of course she was right. What if I'd seriously hurt myself? Knocked myself out of the game forever, just to prove something to some stupid girl and her friends—whose opinions shouldn't even matter.

"If you concentrate on your recovery and you take your time, I have no doubt you'll eventually get back to where you once were," Coach Basil said. "It may set you back a year. Maybe two years—who knows? And along the way you'll have people tell you you're not going to make it. That you're taking too long, that you're missing too many opportunities. But you have to force yourself to ignore all the noise. Concentrate on listening to your own body instead and what it's telling you. When you're ready, you'll know." She smiled. "And then you can show them all."

I felt the tears spring to my eyes. I opened my mouth to reply but found I couldn't form the words. But Coach

Basil only smiled again, pulling me into her arms and giving me a warm hug.

"I believe in you," she whispered. "You can do this."

At that moment, as if on cue, the music swelled, and my own voice came belting out over the air in a perfect tune of solidarity and hope. Coach Basil pulled away from the hug, glancing over at the laptop with a knowing grin.

"You know," she said a little impishly. "Music *has* been shown to have great healing properties." She paused. "I mean, just saying."

I stared at her. "You're saying I should join the band?"

"I'm saying . . ." She rose to her feet, heading for the door. When she reached it, she paused, then turned back to me and gestured to my laptop. "You should burn me a copy of this. It'd make a stellar addition to my collection."

I grinned back at her, my heart soaring. For the first time in forever I felt a shred of hope. "I think I can make that happen."

CHAPTER NINETEEN

Five days later and I found myself staring down into Baby Bear, my heart pounding in my chest as I struggled to suck ice-cold air into my lungs. The trainer they'd assigned me was a new guy—transferred from our sister school out west—and not someone I'd known from before. Which was good, I supposed. At least he wouldn't know how far I'd fallen from grace.

I have nothing to prove to anyone, I reminded myself, remembering Coach Basil's words.

After our talk I'd decided to take the week off, telling my dad I needed time to get back into the swing of things—get caught up on my schoolwork and better adjusted to life on the mountain again. He hadn't liked it, but Coach Basil, true to her word, had backed me up, and he'd eventually given his okay.

So Monday through Thursday I did just that. Went to school in the morning, then went back to my dorm and studied in the afternoons while everyone else was out on the slopes. Okay, I admit some of that so-called studying might have involved Manic Pixie lyrics and melodies—and singing along to the recordings Coach Basil had let me download from her iPod. I was still too chicken to actually text Scarlet and Lulu and tell them I wanted to join the band, but I did follow the band's Instagram so I could keep in the loop. And soon I found myself looking forward to everyone heading out to the mountain so I could score some solo singing time.

Not to mention time to talk to Logan. He'd text me when he got home from school and he didn't have to work, and we'd play games online or just chat back and forth. And the more I learned about him, the more I liked him. He was sweet. Silly. Encouraging. Saturday couldn't come soon enough.

But Friday came first. And weirdly, I found myself waking up, longing for snow. It was as if my body was telling me it was ready, just as Coach Basil had predicted.

So I went with it. Called up my trainer and asked him to meet me on the mountain. I was ready to rock this thing.

Except now, looking down, I wasn't so sure anymore. My heart started to struggle to the beat of a different drum, sending waves of anxiety to the tips of my fingers and toes while my mind raced with horrifying visions of cracked wrists and broken ankles.

"Are you okay?" my trainer asked, peering at me with concern.

I gave him a distracted nod, trying to concentrate on the techniques the nurse had taught me after my first panic attack. Deep breaths. Slow, deep breaths to calm my racing pulse and lower my heart rate. Pushing away the haunting visions of my accident and filling my mind with happy thoughts instead.

Like thoughts of Logan, for example. His goofy smile. His threats of a snowball assault if I didn't find a way to have good time.

I think you're awesome, he'd said. *And who are they to tell me I'm wrong?*

"What's so funny?" my trainer interrupted, jerking me from my thoughts. I looked up, startled.

"What?"

He laughed. "You're just standing there, grinning like a loon. Did I miss some joke?"

"Oh." I blushed. "No, I'm just . . . thinking of something nice."

"That's good," he said approvingly. "Positive thoughts are important. Just let me know when you're ready and we can go. No rush."

"Okay." I turned back to the mountain, forcing myself to look down . . .

. . . and all happy thoughts flew from my head in a flash of light.

"Um," I stammered. I knew the trail below wasn't the least bit steep, yet somehow it suddenly seemed a cavernous abyss. "Um, yeah. One sec, okay?"

Come on, Lexi. I bit my lower lip. *Think of Logan, think of Logan.*

But as the wind whipped at my face, I realized that wasn't enough. And the fear once again threatened to consume me. Not the fear that I couldn't get down this particular slope, this particular time. But that I would never be able to get down any slopes ever again.

On some level I knew that didn't make any sense— after all, I'd been down several trails with Logan the

198

weekend before and it seemed logical that I could do it again. But at this point, all logic had gone out the window and the panic rose inside of me at a frightening rate. My chest tightened, the pressure mounting. I frantically wondered if my trainer would be as understanding as Logan had been if I told him I wanted to ride the chair lift back down the mountain.

No, I scolded myself. *That's not going to happen this time. No matter what it takes. You just need something to distract you. To get your mind off all the crazy.*

But what? What could possibly distract me all the way down the mountain? Counting? Solving math problems in my head? I was never very good at math to begin with—that might only make things worse. But what else? What else was I good at? Besides snowboarding, of course. And how ironic was that?

My head shot up. "Do you mind if I sing?" I asked the trainer, feeling more than a little embarrassed at the suggestion. But singing had helped me once upon a time, back when I was still competing. Maybe it could still help now.

He looked a little taken aback. Then he grinned. "As long as you don't expect me to join in. My voice pretty much has the power to break glass. And not in a good way."

"Fair enough," I agreed, sucking in a breath. Gathering up my nerves, I started humming my favorite Manic Pixie tune. Softly at first.

Then adding volume.

Then words.

When I got to the chorus, I pushed off.

Down the mountain I went. Singing at the top of my lungs.

I'm not going to tell you it was my best run ever. Or that I suddenly showed mad skills or speed. But somehow, through sheer force of music, I guess, I made it to the bottom. Right now, for me, that was something.

In fact, it was a lot.

And the next trail we faced, I didn't hesitate quite so long at the top. I just sang and thought of Logan and the band, and soon the exhilaration of racing down the mountain managed to drown out my last remaining fear.

Until, that was, I fell.

I still don't know exactly how it happened. Maybe I hit a patch of bare ice. Maybe I lost focus, a little too wrapped up in my song. In any case I suddenly found myself losing my edge, my board slipping out from under me and flipping into the air, sending me down to the earth below.

I hit the ground hard, the impact of my helmet against the ice sending shockwaves through my head and down my backbone. I tried to dig in my edge, but the ice was too slick, and I found myself sliding uncontrollably down the mountain, my heart racing as fast as my body.

By the time gravity released me at a dip in the trail, I was crying my eyes out, pounding the snow furiously.

"It's not fair!" I screamed to no one. "This is so not fair."

I knew I wasn't seriously hurt. It was just a fall—like a thousand I'd had before. But somehow it felt different. As if my body was saying, *I told you so.*

What if I never got past this? What if I never got back to where I was? What if my father was wrong—that I couldn't return to my former glory? What if Golden Girl was gone for good?

"No!" I cried involuntarily, my voice echoing up the mountain. "I won't let you win!" I struggled to my feet, just as my trainer reached me.

"Are you okay?" he asked, peering at me with concern.

"I'm fine," I declared, with more bravado than I felt. "Let's go."

Not waiting for his reply, I pushed myself off again, picking up my song where I'd left it. Louder this time. More forcibly. Practically screaming out the words.

Somehow I got down the mountain. And I didn't fall again.

The trainer caught up to me at the chairlift line. He clapped me on the shoulder. "That's the way to do it," he said. "Do you want to go again?"

I stared down at my feet, still strapped to the board. The old me would have said, *Oh yeah*. I was going to board until my feet bled just to prove I still had what it took. But I was exhausted, I realized. Still shaky. Still scared. And I remembered Coach Basil's words.

Listen to what your body's telling you.

I leaned down and unstrapped the board from my feet. "I need a break," I told my trainer. "But let's meet up again this afternoon. I'll be ready to go again by then."

CHAPTER TWENTY

My instincts proved correct, and after a nice long lunch break, I was ready to head out to the mountain again, and I have to say, the afternoon session ended up even better than the morning one. Sure, I fell a few more times—but I always got back up, each time managing to keep the panic at bay. By the time the lifts closed for the afternoon, I was feeling more confident than ever.

Once I put my board away in the school ski lockers, I headed across campus toward the dorm, figuring I'd have time to shower and change before meeting up with Brooklyn and Caitlin and the gang for movie night in the lounge. On the way I found myself wandering past the half-pipe where I'd first met Logan, and my pulse kicked up with excitement. Tomorrow I'd get to see him again. I couldn't wait to tell him all that I'd accomplished. He was going to be so proud of me.

I was so caught up in my dreamy thoughts, I almost tripped over a figure crouched in the snow. "Oh! I'm sorry!" I cried, stumbling backward. "I didn't see—"

My eyes widened as I realized who it was. "Becca?" What was she doing down there on the ground?

"Leave me alone."

Her voice choked on the words, and I realized she was crying. I dropped to my knees and gave her a thorough once-over. Was she hurt? Had she fallen on the pipe? Visions of my own accident danced through my head as I examined her for possible injuries.

"What's wrong?" I asked after finding nothing obvious. "Are you okay?"

My former best friend slammed a bare fist in the snow. I cringed, noticing her raw, red fingers. "I'm fine," she sputtered, sounding anything but.

I frowned. "You don't look fine."

"I don't care what I look like."

"Come on, Becca," I pleaded. "It's me. Lexi."

Becca looked up, her eyes darting around the base

lodge. Finally, as if convinced we were indeed alone, and no one was going to report her for speaking with the enemy, she turned back to me. "I'm just sick of being so bad," she admitted. "Seriously, I don't know what's wrong with me these days. I practice all the time. And yet I still stink. I don't deserve to be here. They should kick me out and send me back to public school."

"What are you talking about?" I asked, honestly confused. "You so don't stink." Well, maybe lately she'd been stinking as a best friend, but I wasn't about to go there. After all, maybe this was my chance. A chance to remind her that I was there for her—no matter what. "And you definitely deserve to be here at Mountain Academy. You're one of the best snowboard crossers we have here."

"Yeah, well, tell that to Coach Merkin," Becca muttered, staring back down at her feet. "He said I have to get my time down by at least ten seconds if I want to stay on the team." She kicked at the snow with her boot. "But I've been running the course all day and I can't seem to find those ten seconds, no matter what I do. And now my knee is killing me." She rubbed the joint in question for emphasis. I grimaced, knowing all too well the pain she must be in.

"Well, you'll never do it if you're all stressed out like this," I told her. "In fact, it's a good way to get yourself hurt." Funny, I never would have given that advice before my accident. But now it made perfect sense.

Becca scrubbed her face with her hands. "I don't have a choice," she protested. "I can't get dropped from the team. My parents will kill me."

"Come on," I declared, an idea coming to me. I rose to my feet and held out a hand to her. "I'm taking you on a field trip."

She looked at me as if I had sprouted three heads. "I can't go on a field trip," she protested. "I have to practice."

"The lifts are closed. You can practice tomorrow. And I'm willing to bet you'll do a whole lot better if you take a break first," I argued, not willing to take no for an answer. I finally had a chance to help Becca—to show her how much I cared about her—and I wasn't going to let it slip away. I just prayed Olivia didn't pick that moment to show up and cause Becca to go all weird on me again.

Becca bit her lower lip, obviously contemplating. I held my breath, waiting to see what she'd decide. Finally she let out a long sigh and took my hand. "Fine," she said in a clipped voice. "But I need to get back before nine. I have a conference call with my parents and the coach about my future."

"No problem," I agreed, ecstatic she'd actually said yes. "Now come on!"

After hitting the lockers to stash Becca's board and change clothes, I led her down to the parking lot and toward the bus stop. I was so excited it was all I could do not to bounce up and down with joy. Me and Becca, one on one, just like the old days. And where we were going, Olivia would never be able to bust her.

"Where on earth are you taking me?" Becca asked, sounding curious despite herself as the bus chugged up the hill toward our stop, black smoke puffing from its rear exhaust. I remembered the first time I got on the bus; I was just as weirded out. But I couldn't spoil the surprise.

"Trust me," I said, flashing her a grin.

To her credit, she did, though she still looked a little doubtful as we boarded the bus and took our seats. The vehicle pulled around, out of the resort and down the hill, toward Littleton.

"Aren't we going to get in trouble for leaving campus?" she asked, peering out the grimy window.

"Not if we don't get caught."

About ten minutes later the bus pulled up to the same intersection where Logan and I had exited the time before. I remembered how nervous I was then; now I was just as excited. Becca followed me doubtfully off the bus, her gaze flicking from side to side. But I just grabbed her hand and dragged her on until we reached Bill's.

"A bar?" she asked, looking up at the buzzing neon letters with questions in her eyes.

"Coffee house," I corrected, pushing open the door. I turned, wanting to see her reaction as she stepped inside.

Sure enough, her jaw dropped as she scanned the room, taking in all the old-fashioned video games. It was early, and the place was pretty much deserted, save for Bill the pirate barista behind the bar.

"Whoa!" Becca cried. "What is this place?" She skipped over to the Pac-Man machine, wrapping her hand around the joystick. "These are like totally ancient!" she exclaimed, abandoning the game for the Centipede machine next to it. "And the graphics are horrible!" She turned to me, her face shining. "And completely awesome!"

I reached into my pocket and pulled out the handful

of quarters I'd been stashing in my locker all week, depositing them into her palm. "Go have fun," I instructed firmly. "And don't even think about snowboarding for the next hour."

Becca didn't argue, slipping a quarter into the Gauntlet machine, then gesturing for me to join her. Before long, my elf and her sorceress were downing skeletons by the dozen in a never-ending dungeon quest for treasure and glory.

"Yeah, baby!" Becca cheered as we heroically cleared level thirteen. "Epic win!" She reached over and high-fived me, her eyes dancing with excitement.

As the late afternoon dipped into evening, we battled killer bees, raging robots, dreadful dragons, until our hands grew tired from mashing buttons and gripping joysticks. Exhausted, I stepped back from the Dragon's Lair machine, only to slam into someone behind me. I whirled around, surprised to see Roland, his arms full of cables.

"Lexi!" he cried as he recognized me. "You're here! Are you singing with us tonight?" He dropped the cables and gave me a big bear hug. I hugged him back, excited to see him, too. Even though we didn't know each other well, I'd been listening to his guitar playing in my headphones all week long, making me feel close to him in a weird way.

"Nah. I just brought my friend Becca down for some stress relief," I told him. "I didn't know you guys would be here."

"Yeah, it's open mic night tonight," Roland informed me after glancing at his watch. "Starts in about an hour. Lulu and Scarlet are going to totally freak if they see you. You'd better hide unless you plan to perform with us. You know what they think about taking no for an answer."

"Perform?" Becca asked curiously, coming up behind me.

"Um, long story," I muttered, feeling my face heat.

"What, you didn't know your friend here is the most amazing singer in all of Vermont and maybe New England, too?" Roland asked, smiling at her. "We've made her an honorary member of Manic Pixie Dream Girl."

Becca stared at him, then at me. "I knew you liked to sing in the shower—but in a band?" Then her eyes grew wide. "Wait, Manic Pixie Dream Girl? Isn't that the band Coach Basil was playing in her room the other day? The one everyone was freaking out about and demanding a copy?"

Now I was blushing furiously. "I don't know. Maybe?"

Traitor Coach Basil! That was supposed to be on the down-low!

Related: *Everyone was freaking out? Everyone wanted a copy?*

Becca grabbed my hands, jumping up and down. "Dude! You're like a total rock star!"

"I jammed with them once!" I protested, yanking my hands away. "Trust me, I'm so not a rock star!"

"You could be if you joined us tonight . . . ," Roland said with a waggle of his eyebrows.

I shook my head, reality settling back in. "I can't. I have to get Becca back for her conference call at nine."

My friend groaned. "Forget the conference call! They can reschedule. Or have it without me. That's how they make all their decisions about my life anyway." She rolled her eyes. "Seriously, Lex. When are you going to ever have a chance like this again? You have to go for it!"

I sighed. She wasn't going to give up, was she? "Okay, fine." I relented at last, feeling secretly pleased at the idea. "I guess I could sing. I have been practicing the songs, actually. I mean, just for fun."

"This is awesome!" Roland cried. "The girls are going to totally freak out." He beamed at me. "I'm going to go tell them the good news."

My stomach flip-flopped as I watched him go. I wasn't so sure about this being a good idea. But the shiny excitement on Becca's face made me at least want to try.

CHAPTER TWENTY-ONE

And that was how, about an hour later, I found myself being pushed onstage by Scarlet and Lulu—a microphone placed in my hand. My whole body shook as I looked out over the coffee house and all the people sitting in folding chairs, waiting for us to start. It was probably only a dozen or so, but it might as well have been millions. And the fear that rose to my throat felt like it was trying to choke me.

It was one thing to sing to myself while riding down a mountainside on my board. Another to sing by a fire, accompanied by friends. But it was something else entirely to get onstage in front of an entire audience of strangers and dare to do something I wasn't quite sure I even knew how to do properly.

"I don't know if I can do this," I hissed at Scarlet as she took her place beside me. "What if I mess it up?"

"Then you mess it up," she shot back, not missing a beat. "It's not the end of the world."

"I know, but . . ." I looked out over the crowd of people, my heart beating rapidly in my chest. "I don't want to let you guys down."

"Are you kidding? If you weren't here, we'd have to have Roland sing!" Lulu laughed. "Now *that* would be a letdown."

"Look. It's open mic night at some silly café. Not an *American Idol* audition," Scarlet added. "Seriously, you just need to let it go and have fun. That's it. No one's expecting anything more from you."

It was funny—it was the same advice Logan had given me the weekend before when we'd been snowboarding at Snow Peak. *Let it go. Have fun.* Was I really so uptight that I couldn't do anything in life without turning it into a competitive event? I had nothing to prove to these people. I wasn't looking for a career in music. I had come here tonight to have a good time. To relieve my stress—not bring about more.

It was then I saw Becca, sitting in the front row,

clapping her hands together and whistling loudly. Her eyes were bright and excited. For the first time in a while, I felt like she was on my side.

Suddenly the words from above the archway at school came raging back to me.

What would you attempt to do if you knew you could not fail?

I smiled to myself. I knew very well that I could fail. But I wasn't about to let that stop me this time.

I brought the microphone to my lips. "Hello, Littleton!" I cried. "I'm Alexis Miller. And this is Manic Pixie Dream Girl!"

"Oh my gosh, Lexi, you were so amazing!" Becca squealed for the thousandth time as we boarded the bus on the way back to Mountain Academy. I laughed as my friend danced down the aisle, belting out the chorus to one of the songs. She got a few dirty looks from the other passengers, but she just laughed them off.

"Ladies and gentlemen!" she announced to the entire bus. "Live and in person, this night only! Alexis Miller! Rock star extraordinaire!"

I shoved her playfully into her seat "You do this back

at school and I'll kill you!" I swore as we took our seats. Though I had to admit, it felt pretty good. I had totally rocked the open mic, and I knew it. All that practice had paid off. As the bus pulled away, I could still hear the audience's applause echoing in my ears. I was sure to remember this night for years to come. And I was glad Becca had been there to experience it with me. Just like old times.

"Everyone at school is going to be so jealous that I got to see you live," Becca replied, pulling her phone from her bag and scanning through the pictures she took. "You know, this one would be a perfect profile pic."

"No way." I grabbed the phone from her and deleted the close-up of me onstage. "It's bad enough that Coach Basil is playing the demo for people. If anyone found out we snuck off school grounds—never mind me singing in a band—we'd both get suspended."

"Hey!" Becca grabbed back her phone. "You were the one who said you can't perform well under pressure. I bet singing onstage tonight makes you ten times the snowboarder tomorrow."

I grinned. "I hope you're right. But still, let's still keep this whole thing off social media, just to be safe?"

Becca nodded resolutely. "Thanks for taking me," she said. "I really needed that." She fell silent for a moment, staring out the window. "I guess I've just been feeling the pressure lately, you know? If I don't practice, I won't win. If I don't win . . ." She trailed off.

"If you don't win, you don't win," I replied with a shrug, surprising myself, even as the words spilled from my lips. "It's not the end of the world."

Becca turned and looked at me sharply. "Um, who are you and what did you do with my best friend?"

She was right, of course. Before my accident, winning was everything to me. Nothing mattered beyond the mountain. Snowboarding was my reason to get up in the morning. My reason to live. But now, to be perfectly honest, it seemed . . . less important . . . somehow. Not that I didn't love it. But I was starting to love other things too. And that was okay. In fact, that was a good thing.

But that wasn't what I wanted to talk about now.

"Best friend, huh?" I pointed out quietly. "To be honest, I didn't even think I was your friend anymore."

Becca's face fell. She turned back to the window. But I wasn't giving up so easily. This might be the last chance I had to get her completely alone. I wasn't about to waste it.

"I've missed you, you know," I told her. "It's not the same without you."

She was silent for a moment, and at first I was sure she wasn't going to answer. But then she turned to me, her eyes brimming with unshed tears. "I've missed you, too," she whispered. "And I know I've been a rotten friend lately. I'm really sorry. It's just . . . well . . . complicated. And I . . ."

Unfortunately, at that moment the bus pulled up at our stop, and the doors creaked open. Worst timing ever. I reluctantly rose from my seat and headed down the aisle, Becca following slowly behind me. We said good-bye to the driver and stepped out into the night.

Once the bus had driven away, I turned back to Becca. "What were you saying?" I asked, not willing to let it drop.

Her face turned bright red. "Oh—nothing," she stammered. "I'm just sorry, is all."

Try as I might, I couldn't get anything else out of her. Eventually I just gave up talking altogether. We trudged in silence back toward the school, all the fun of the evening evaporating the closer we got to the gates. It was as if we'd stepped into a dream world for the evening, and now it was time to wake up. I watched Becca from the corner of my eye, wondering what on earth was going on with her. She seemed to want to make up with me, but she wasn't willing to even explain why we'd fallen out to begin with. And how did Olivia play into any of this? I still couldn't figure that part out.

"Well, well, well, look who's best friends again!"

Speak of the devil. I whirled around to find Olivia herself standing behind us, dressed in her ridiculous fur coat, arms crossed over her chest. I glanced at Becca, realizing her face had turned stark white, her eyes wide and terrified.

"We just met on the bus!" she blurted out to my surprise. "I wasn't hanging out with her, I swear!"

I stared at Becca in disbelief. What? Was she really going to deny hanging out with me? What was wrong with her? Why was she so afraid of Olivia?

"Really." Olivia pursed her lips, regarding the two of us with skeptical eyes. "And I suppose you just randomly met on the bus carrying the exact same souvenir mugs from the exact same place you *didn't* hang out at together?"

Becca stole a guilty glance down at the Bill's collectible coffee mug she held in her hands. The one she insisted we both buy—to remember my big night. She knew she was busted.

"Look, Olivia," she tried. "It's not what you think."

But Olivia just rolled her eyes. "No, Becca," she sneered. "It's not what *I* think. It's what *Lexi* thinks, right? That's what's important here," she added, her tone ripe with meaning. As if she knew some hidden joke that I didn't.

"What is your problem?" I demanded, whirling around to face Olivia. "Why can't you just leave us alone?" Then I turned back to my friend, my eyes pleading. "Come on, Becca. You're better than this. You don't have to play her games."

Becca stood for a moment. At last she shook her head. "I've—gotta go," she stammered. "I've got that . . . conference call, you know."

"But I thought you already missed . . . ," I started to say, but realized I was speaking to no one. Becca had fled, leaving me alone with Olivia. My eyes narrowed as I took in her smug expression. She's was having a field day at my expense.

220

"I don't know what is going on," I snapped. "But I'm going to find out."

Olivia laughed, reaching into her pocket for a piece of gum. She popped it into her mouth. "Don't look too hard, Golden Girl," she purred. "You might not like what you find."

CHAPTER TWENTY-TWO

"Argh, she just makes me so mad!" I growled, slamming my fork down at dinner the next day. I had taken the bus to meet Logan, and we'd caught a movie, then headed to Bill's, where I'd spent the last hour hanging out with Scarlet and Lulu and Roland, singing with the band. I felt more confident after Coach Basil's pep talk—not to mention last night's performance, and though I knew I was still a total noob, the whole thing was so much fun that I no longer minded messing up from time to time. And none of my bandmates held it against me when I did.

Once band practice was over, Logan took me to this cute little diner a few blocks away that looked straight out of a 1950s sitcom. I ordered an extra-large chocolate milk shake and a grilled cheese sandwich with fries. And let me tell you, to me it tasted better than any prime filet at Jacques's.

Logan gave me a sympathetic look. I sighed.

"I'm sorry," I said. "Here I've been waiting all week to see you, and now I'm just complaining."

He smiled at me. "It's okay," he said. "I'd be mad too." He picked up his burger. "That girl sounds like nothing but trouble."

"Seriously. I mean, you'd think after the whole race thing she'd be sitting pretty. But no. She's still working overtime to make sure my life is ruined in every possible way. Girl needs a hobby, for real."

Logan cocked his head in question. "Wait—what race thing?"

I looked up. I'd forgotten he didn't know. But of course he didn't. No one did.

Suddenly I had the overwhelming urge to tell him everything. Since I'd gotten back to Mountain Academy, the secret had been weighing heavier and heavier on my heart each day. I desperately wanted to tell someone. So why not Logan? He wasn't involved. He had nothing to lose or gain and no one to tell. Besides, I was pretty sure he was the type of guy who would keep a girl's secret—even under torture.

I thought back to Olivia's smug smile outside the school the night before. Becca's fearful eyes. I had once believed that by keeping the truth about my "accident" a secret it would save my best friend's career. Had I somehow made things worse for her instead?

"You have to promise not to say anything," I blurted out. "To anyone."

He nodded, his expression grave. I could tell he was taking me seriously, and I appreciated that.

So I told him everything. The words coming hesitantly at first, then spilling over my lips like water from a burst dam. Logan listened, attentively, silently, with no readable expression on his face. Only the knuckles whitening in his clenched fists gave anything away.

"Geez, Lexi," he murmured when I had finished. "I knew Mountain Academy was competitive. But that . . ." He shook his head. "She should be banned from the sport forever . . . or at least kicked out of school."

"I'm sure she didn't mean to hurt me that badly," I protested. "She was just trying to slow me down so she could get ahead."

"Oh. Well that makes it all better then."

I grimaced. "I know, I know. I'm not trying to defend her. She's an abominable snow brat; believe me, I get it. But what can I do?"

"You could go to the school. Or the cops. Or . . . something."

"I can't," I said. "Even if I wanted to, I don't have any proof. And they'd want to know why I didn't say something back when it happened. It'd be her word against mine, and her dad owns the stupid mountain." I paused, then added, "Besides, I couldn't do that to Becca."

He raised an eyebrow. "Olivia's minion, Becca?"

I groaned. "You don't understand. Becca isn't like that. She's a good person. She works really hard, and she doesn't buy into all that popularity stuff. There's something else going on with her, I know it. Like Olivia's holding something over her head. But I can't for the life of me figure out what it could be. I wish I could—I'm sure if I just knew what it was I could make her see it was no big deal."

Logan thought about this for a moment. "We could see if Todd knows," he suggested.

"Todd?" I frowned. "As in Olivia's boyfriend, Todd?"

"Ex-boyfriend," Logan corrected. "He broke up with her last Saturday. Pretty much right after we ran into them."

"What?" I exclaimed, surprised. "Why?"

Logan shrugged. "Evidently she started saying a bunch of stuff about me being a staff rat and he got mad. Todd's not rich, you know. He's a scholarship kid from the Bronx."

Golden Boy was on scholarship? I had no idea. And I was pretty sure none of the other kids did either. Obviously Olivia didn't or she'd never deem him worthy enough for her princessdom.

"Anyway, they got into a fight and he cut her loose. Told me it was for the best. Said she was kind of a psycho." He blew out a long breath. "Until now I had no idea just how psycho he meant."

"Wow," I said, remembering the dinner at Jacques's. I had thought Olivia was acting a little crazy, even for her. "And now she probably blames me for getting dumped, on top of everything else. Awesome."

"In any case, we should go and ask him about the whole Becca thing," Logan suggested. "He might know something."

"It's worth a try."

226

. . .

Logan insisted on coming along with me to talk to Todd, even though he was technically still banned from the mountain, and an hour later we were knocking on the snowboarder's dorm room door. Todd answered dressed in jeans and a ratty Minecraft T-shirt. He grinned when he saw Logan.

"Hey, man." He greeted Logan, slapping him on the arm. "Come on in."

We entered the dorm room and sat down on Todd's roommate's unoccupied bed. I looked around: On the walls hung posters of all the snowboarding greats and one of skateboarder Tony Hawk. Todd's trophies and medals covered the top of his dresser in a sea of gold, and a trash bin overflowed with empty cans of Red Bull.

Todd plopped down on his desk chair, leaning forward, elbows on his knees. "So, Miss Miller, to what do I owe the pleasure of this visit?"

I drew in a breath. "Do you know Becca Montgomery?"

"Sure. Olivia's latest lamebrain. What about her?"

I frowned, not appreciating his description of my poor friend. "She's not—"

"We think Olivia might be blackmailing her," Logan

cut in quickly. "Like she has something on her that Becca doesn't want people to know."

Todd laughed. "Of course she does. Olivia has stuff on everyone in school. It's like her hobby. Some people collect baseball cards. She collects secrets."

"Do you know what she might have on Becca?" I asked, leaning forward anxiously.

But Todd just shook his head. "Sorry," he said. "She didn't mention anything that I can think of. Or that I remember, anyway. No offense, but that girl never shuts up. Half of what she said went in one ear and out the other."

"Okay," I said, disappointed. "Well, thanks anyway." I rose to leave.

"Wait," Todd commanded. I stopped in my tracks, turning to him.

"Yeah?"

"I said she didn't *tell* me anything," he said. "Not that we couldn't find out."

I cocked my head in question. "What do you mean?"

"She keeps files on people," he explained. "On her computer. Pretty much everyone she knows has a file." He rolled his eyes. "Yeah, she's really that much of a creeper—I know."

My heart picked up its pace. "And you think she might have a file on Becca?"

"Only one way to find out." Todd swung around in his chair, pulled up to his computer desk, and began typing away furiously.

"Are you going to hack her account?" Everyone at Mountain Academy was given a log-in that could be accessed from any computer on campus. This way you could always pull up your homework or whatever you needed, wherever you were.

"Don't need to. I have her password," he informed us. "Twelve twelve. The date of her mother's death." He turned to look at us. "Morbid, right?"

I thought back to Olivia on the floor outside of Jacques's, crying her eyes out, saying she wished her mother was still alive. It didn't excuse what she'd done, I told myself. But it did make me feel the tiniest bit bad for her. After all, I couldn't imagine something like that happening to my mother. I'm pretty sure I wouldn't even be able to function as a human being for the next ten years, never mind win any races.

A moment later Todd leaned back in his chair, looking pleased with himself. "Okay, here we are."

I peered at the screen. Sure enough, we were on Olivia's desktop. A selfie of her and her mom smiling into the camera wallpapered across the screen. Along with a set of file folders, carefully arranged and labeled with the full names of Mountain Academy students. Wow.

"I don't even want to know what she has on me at this point," Todd laughed as he moused over his own name. He right-clicked and gleefully hit delete. I gave Logan an alarmed look. We were going down a slippery slope, and I knew it.

It's for Becca, I tried to remind myself. *You're doing it for Becca.*

"Here we go," Todd announced a moment later, dragging a folder with Becca's name across the desktop. "Now let's see what she has on your friend."

As he clicked on the folder, my breath caught in my throat. I peered down, not sure I really wanted to see. It had to be something really bad if Becca was willing to give up our entire friendship over it. But what could it possibly be?

I scanned the Word document. A few nasty comments about Becca's wardrobe. A few notes about her recent times on various snowboarding events. A few suggestions to "let her borrow some clothes so she doesn't embarrass us at the next mixer."

"Hmm, nothing incriminating," I remarked, a sinking feeling settling in my stomach. Had I been wrong about Olivia holding something over my friend's head?

"Wait. There's a video," Todd pointed out, clicking on one of the .mov files. A moment later a QuickTime video popped up on the screen and began to play. It appeared to have been taken at some kind of school dance. The camera panned the rec center, focusing on a few Boarder Barbies hanging out on the sidelines, looking bored.

"What does this have to do with Becca?" I wondered aloud. Maybe it had accidentally been placed in the wrong folder?

As if in answer, the camera swung around, exchanging the view of the dance floor for that of a window. Then it zoomed in, focusing on two people outside the rec center.

Two people kissing. One: my should-have-been boyfriend, Cam.

The other: my best friend.

Todd turned to me, raising a questioning eyebrow. "Does this mean anything to you?" he asked.

I couldn't answer. Just stared at the computer screen, rendered speechless.

When had this happened? I reached over Todd to grab the mouse, right-clicking the video file to discover the date. I drew in a horrified breath. It was last year. The very same day of the fateful race that had sent me to the hospital. *The very same dance*, I suddenly realized, that I was supposed to go to with Cam in the first place.

I felt as if I'd been punched in the gut.

"And . . . that's all she wrote," Todd said, turning back to me. "Did you want to look up anyone else while you're here? She has this classic video of Ava slipping on ice and falling flat on her face." He smirked impishly.

"We're good," Logan replied, cuffing him on the shoulder. "I'll catch you later, okay?"

Todd gave him a salute. "Hurry up and get yourself unbanned, dude. I'm bored to tears without someone worthy to race."

Logan gave him a mock salute, then led me out of the room, closing the door behind us. Once we were safely in the hallway, I drew in a huge, shaky breath.

"Are you okay?" Logan asked.

"Yeah," I said, still feeling a little dazed. I quickly explained the backstory so he'd understand what Becca had done.

"Ugh," he said when I'd finished. "That's pretty tacky."

"I know, right?" I exclaimed. "Like here I am, in the hospital, literally fighting for my life, and she's all kissing the guy who was supposed to be my boyfriend. Who does that?" I scowled, squeezing my hands into fists. "I mean, not that I care anymore," I added quickly, not wanting him to think I still had feelings for that slimeball Cam. "Just on principle."

"No, I get it," Logan assured me as we stepped outside into the crisp November evening.

The sun was just starting to set, casting deep shadows across the trails. Logan led me over to a nearby bench, and we both sat down. "She went behind your back. And she lied to you. That's not cool."

"I guess Olivia must have caught them," I added. "She probably threatened to text me the video if Becca didn't do what she said." Suddenly my best friend's behavior was making a lot more sense.

"What are you going to do?" Logan asked.

233

Before I could answer, I caught movement across the way. Looking up, I accidentally made perfect eye contact with none other than Olivia herself. Her eyes narrowed as they caught mine, then she smirked and turned away. As if she had already won. I watched her go, my hands closing into fists again.

"Ugh. Seriously, I just want to smack her upside the head."

"Or . . . you could go make up with Becca," Logan suggested. "Perhaps that would be an even sweeter revenge."

I considered this for a moment, then nodded. "You're right," I agreed. "I'll let her know I saw the video and that it doesn't matter to me. That I forgive her. And that she doesn't have to do Olivia's bidding anymore."

I didn't know if it would work. But to get my best friend back, it was worth a try.

CHAPTER TWENTY-THREE

"Hey, Lex, over here!"

It was Monday morning, and I'd just entered the cafeteria for breakfast. I looked up to see Brooklyn waving me over to our regular table. I forced yet another one of the fake smiles I'd been constantly wearing for the past week and headed over to talk to her.

"How's it going?" she asked. "You going to be joining us again soon?"

"Looks like maybe next week," I told her. "If my trainer gives me the go-ahead."

"Sweet!" Brooklyn cried. She reached across the table to give me a fist bump. "I can't wait for you to start kicking Olivia's butt again. Girl has gotten completely unbearable without you putting her in her place."

"Oh, don't worry," I assured her. "That's definitely on the agenda."

In fact, Operation Take Olivia Down was starting right now. As soon as I could locate Becca.

It didn't take me long to spot her, sitting over at her new usual table with the other Boarder Barbies. I watched, calmly eating my lunch, biding my time, until she rose from her seat and headed out of the cafeteria. I smiled. Middle-of-lunch bathroom break. My former bestie was nothing if not predictable.

"Be right back," I told my crew as I slipped out from behind the bench and headed toward the exit. I kept my steps slow, allowing her enough distance that she wouldn't be able to tell she was being trailed. My heart thudded in my chest as I watched her enter the bathroom, the door swinging shut behind her. This was it. My chance to get her alone and confront her with what I'd learned.

I entered the bathroom and peeked under each and every stall, making sure we were really by ourselves. Then I cleared my throat.

"Becca?"

I watched her feet freeze from behind the stall door.

"Yeah?" she asked, her voice sounding tinny and scared.

"Can we talk?"

For a moment there was silence. But, of course, she knew she didn't have a choice. She couldn't stay in the bathroom forever. Finally, the toilet flushed and the door swung open. Becca emerged looking cagey and wide-eyed. "Sure," she said. "What's up?"

"Look, Becca," I said, putting a hand on her arm. "I don't know how else to do this so I'm just going to come out and say it." I drew in a breath. "I saw the video."

Becca's face drained of all color. Her hands gripped the bathroom counter so hard I could see her knuckles turning white. "How did you . . . ?" she croaked. "I mean . . . what . . . ?" She swallowed hard. "Oh, Lexi."

She looked so devastated. Obviously she was extremely sorry for what she'd done. Giving her my best forgiving smile, I pulled her into my arms and tried to give her a hug. Her body was stiff, and she was shaking like a leaf. Poor thing. She'd been suffering with this secret for way too long. Now she could just let it go.

"It's okay, Becca," I assured her. "I don't even care

about what you did. I mean, sure, I probably wouldn't nominate you for best friend of the year or anything. But—"

She jerked away from the hug, staring at me with a horrified look on her face. "Please don't tell anyone," she begged, her voice hoarse.

"I won't," I assured her, a little confused, to be honest. "But it's really no big deal."

"No big deal? I could be kicked out of school! And if my parents found out . . ."

"What?" I stared at her, now really, really confused. "It was just a kiss! I mean, I know technically we're not supposed to be alone with boys, blah, blah, blah. But there's no way they'd kick you out of school for something so . . ." I trailed off, realizing Becca was staring at me incredulously.

"Are you talking about me and Cam?" she demanded.

"Uh, yeah?" I frowned. "Isn't that what you're talking about? That video of you and him making out outside of the dance after my accident?"

I could see Becca swallow hard. "Everyone knows about that," she protested. "I mean, except you, I guess. But it was no big deal. He was upset cause you wouldn't let anyone visit you while you were at the hospital. I was comforting him. He got the wrong idea. Did you even watch the whole video? The part where I punched him in the face two seconds later? That's why Olivia saved it in the first place. In case he tried to say something—we wanted proof that he deserved what he got."

"Oh." Now I was completely at a loss. If this were true (and I had no reason to believe it wasn't) then why had she acted so scared when I'd first mentioned a video. Was there another video?

"Becca," I said, turning back to her. "When I said—"

Before I could get the words out, the bathroom door burst open. Olivia and two Boarder Barbies sauntered in. She narrowed her eyes at me, then turned to Becca.

"There you are!" she cried. "We were beginning to think you'd fallen in."

Becca's face turned beet red. She shuffled from foot to foot. "I was just—washing my hands," she stammered.

"Well, wash them and let's go," Olivia announced. "We've got important things to do. The boys at table three won't just flirt with themselves you know."

I caught Becca giving me an anguished look.

"You don't have to do what she says, you know," I reminded her softly, even though I was pretty sure, from the look on her face, that it would do no good.

Sure enough, she just shook her head. "You don't understand, Lexi," she said at last. "And if you did, well, I'm pretty sure you wouldn't be asking me to stay."

CHAPTER TWENTY-FOUR

I stared at the computer screen after dinner, my heart pounding in my chest as my fingers hovered over the keys. Did I really want to do this? It was breaking all sorts of rules. In fact, I could probably even get expelled from school. But what choice did I have? I had to know what Olivia was holding over Becca. If it wasn't the Cam thing, it had to be something else.

I drew in a breath. Then I typed in her password.

The page loaded, and I soon found myself viewing Olivia's desktop, the picture of her and her mom at the bottom of the half-pipe stretching across the screen. It didn't take me long to find and select Becca's folder, and I forced myself to click it open, as apprehension coursed through my veins.

But the fear soon simmered to disappointment as I checked out each and every file. The same files that had been there before. Nothing new. Nothing incriminating. Nothing to give Olivia power over my friend.

Frustrated, I moved to sign out of the account. But before I could, the dorm room door swung open. I looked behind me guiltily as I saw Caitlin step into the room.

"What are you looking at?" she asked curiously, crossing the room and peering over my shoulder before I could close out of anything. "What's that? What are all those names? And why do you have a picture of Olivia on your computer?"

I sighed, deciding to come clean. "Do you promise not to tell anyone?"

"Of course!"

I wasn't a hundred percent sure I believed her, but I felt the need to tell someone, and she was the only one available. "Fine," I said. "I'm logged into Olivia's desktop. I was trying to figure out if she had something on Becca that was making her act so weird." I sighed. "But there's nothing there. Nothing! I just don't get it. I mean, did you know Cam kissed Becca?"

Caitlin grinned. "Yes! And then she punched him in the face!"

I sighed, staring at the photo of Olivia and her mom. "I just don't get it," I repeated. Then I shook my head. "Oh well. I guess that's it." I made a move to close the window again.

"Wait a sec! She has files on everyone? What about me?" Caitlin asked, grabbing the mouse from my hand. She clicked the folder to make the files list alphabetically. But there was no Caitlin in the C section.

"What? Come on, Olivia!" she cried. "I don't even warrant a brief mention?" She looked so offended I had to laugh.

"Do you *want* her to have something on you?"

"Duh! It would make me feel so scandalous." She snorted. "Did you look at *your* file? I can't even imagine the dirt she's got on you."

"I don't want to know."

Caitlin gave me a skeptical look. "Seriously? You aren't even the least bit curious?"

Okay, I was. In fact, suddenly I was insanely curious and wondered why it hadn't occurred to me to look before now. As I grabbed the mouse from her and guided

243

it over to my name, Caitlin let out an excited squeak. I shot her a warning look. "Remember what I told you," I reminded her.

"It stays in the vault," my roommate assured me, holding up her fingers in a Girl Scout–style salute.

I clicked on the folder and it opened.

"Whoa," Caitlin breathed as the files revealed themselves. Unlike Becca's folder, which contained only a few items, my folder was packed to the brim. Newspaper articles about my wins, articles about my losses. Stuff about the accident. Olivia had collected it all.

"Dude, that's creepy," my roommate declared. "It's like she's totally obsessed with you!"

"Yeah," I said, scrolling through the files, feeling more and more sick to my stomach. My mouse hovered over a .mov file, and I swallowed hard. She had a video of me, too? My mind flashed to the open mic night at Bill's. Becca had taken a bunch of pictures and video. Had she then handed them over to my enemy for future blackmail purposes?

I clicked on the video. I had to know for sure.

But as the player loaded up and the video started to play, I realized it wasn't of me singing at all.

"Dude," Caitlin cried. "Is that what I think it is?"

I stared at the screen in disbelief. Watching a scene straight out of my nightmares. A shaky home video of that fateful day on the snowboard cross course when Olivia had unofficially attempted to ruin my life.

"Why would she keep this?" I asked, watching, horrified, as the camera panned across the course. "I mean, why would she want evidence lying around of what she did to me?"

Caitlin looked at me, confused. "Wait, what did she do?"

I sighed, pressing pause on the video. "You have to promise never to tell anyone."

"I already promised, remember? Geez, do you want it written in blood?"

It wasn't a bad idea, actually, but I decided to tell her anyway. What did it matter at this point? There was a video. An actual video.

"Are you serious?" Caitlin cried when I had finished. "I mean, I knew Olivia was crazy, but that's like 'go directly to jail, do not pass go,' crazy. Why didn't you say something?"

"It's a long story," I muttered. I dragged my mouse

back to the video, and I wondered if I should just delete it and be done with it forever. But that would be a mistake, I realized. Because now I had something to use against Olivia. Something to ruin her life if she tried again to ruin mine. I didn't want to have to stoop to her level. But I wanted to keep the option open, just in case.

I unpaused the video. The camera panned up the mountain, revealing Olivia, Becca, and me racing down the slope. I was in a good position, right between my two competitors. We got closer and closer. I watched as I bent my knees, readying myself for—

I squeezed my eyes shut, unable to watch as we came barreling toward the lip of the jump. I knew what was going to happen, and the last thing I wanted to do was to see—

"Oh my gosh!" Caitlin screeched.

"What?" I forced my eyes open, just in time to treat myself to a vision of year-ago me crashing into the old oak tree.

"Argh!" I cried, throwing my hands over my eyes again. "I can't watch this!" My stomach rolled, and I was this close to throwing up. "Stop the video! Please."

Caitlin reached over and stopped it. I opened my

eyes to see a freeze-frame of me, on the ground, clutching my knee, sobbing pitifully. I quickly switched off the monitor, swallowing back the nausea.

"Did you see it?" I asked in a trembling voice. "Did you see Olivia do it?" My heart pounded in my chest as I waited for her confirmation.

"Um." Caitlin shuffled from foot to foot, refusing to meet my eyes. Fear started thrumming through my veins, but I wasn't sure why.

"What?" I asked, confused. "What's wrong? Couldn't you see it happen?" Maybe the angle had been wrong. Or someone had stepped in the way.

"I saw it," Caitlin said in a tight voice that sounded nothing like her own. "Believe me, I saw it."

I swallowed hard. "You saw Olivia grab my jacket?"

"No." She shook her head. "I saw Becca do it."

CHAPTER TWENTY-FIVE

hat?" I asked, obviously having heard her wrong. "What did you just say?"

"Lexi . . ." Caitlin's face was pained.

"No!" I cried. "You must have seen it wrong." I switched the monitor back on and grabbed the mouse, moving the pointer back over to the video. There had to be some mistake. Obviously. Because any alternative would be completely absurd. Becca grabbing my jacket? Becca destroying my life? Becca had been my best friend. There was absolutely no way Becca would ever—

Then I remembered Becca's terrified face in the bathroom. When I told her I'd seen the video. Of course I'd meant the video of her kissing Cam. But she'd meant . . . something else entirely.

"I'm so sorry, Lex," Caitlin was saying as the video started playing again. She pressed a hand to my back, but I shrugged it off, my eyes glued to the screen as the three of us came racing down the hill again. I didn't want to watch. I really didn't want to watch. But I forced my eyes to stay focused on the screen. I had to know.

Even though, deep down, I already did.

"Stop it," I managed to choke out somehow after it was all said and done. "Stop the video."

I felt as if I'd been punched in the stomach, and it was all I could do to not throw up then and there. Becca was my friend. She'd never do something like this. This was the kind of thing Olivia did to people. Not Becca. Not my best friend Becca.

"Maybe it was an accident," I whispered, sinking down onto the floor. It was all I could do, at that point, not to curl up in a fetal position as everything started sliding into a sick sense of place. Olivia must have been holding this over Becca's head all year long. Threatening to go public if Becca didn't do what she said. Get her kicked out of school, maybe land her in juvenile detention . . .

"An accident?" I could feel Caitlin's incredulous stare.

"Lexi, come on. How could someone just accidentally grab someone's jacket and yank them down like that?"

She was right. I knew she was right. There was no denying it now; we'd both seen the whole thing caught on video. Besides, if it had been an accident somehow, wouldn't Becca have admitted it right away? Told everyone what had happened and forfeited the race? Instead, she'd gone on to win and take first place. Scoring a spot on the team and two new sponsors, all while I was being rushed to the ER.

"Why, Becca?" I yelled to no one, stumbling over to my bed and throwing myself down on my pillow. "Why would you do something like that? To me!"

Caitlin climbed onto the bed next to me, pulling me into a hug. For a moment we just lay there. Even cheerful Caitlin could think of nothing positive to say in a moment like this.

"What are you going to do?" she asked at last. "Are you going to tell your dad? Or go straight to the school board?"

"Maybe I shouldn't do anything," I said slowly. "I mean, what's done is done; it won't change anything, right?"

Caitlin jerked up. "Are you insane?" she cried. "She

hurt you! Like, really bad! You can't just let her get away with it."

I stared up at the ceiling, not knowing what to say. I thought about what would happen if the whole thing went public. Sure, it would destroy Becca's life, and maybe she deserved that. But what about me? People had finally stopped treating me like an accident victim. Finally stopped bringing the whole thing up in casual conversation. But once this was out there—it would start all over again. Everyone would be talking about it. Everyone would be looking at me with pitying eyes.

Poor Lexi. Sabotaged by her best friend.

I'd have to go before the school board. What if I had to testify in court? I didn't know if I could deal with that on top of everything else that was going on. I wanted to recover, to move on, to forget it ever happened. Not bring it all raging back with a vengeance.

I slipped off the bed and walked over to the computer. I stuck a thumb drive into the USB port and copied the video onto it. Then I deleted it from Olivia's files and closed out of her account.

"I'm going to hold on to this for now," I told Caitlin. "Until I decide what to do." At least this way it would keep the decision in my hands. Under my control. And Olivia wouldn't have anything else to hold over Becca's head.

Unless, of course, there were other copies lying around. But I couldn't think about that now.

Caitlin frowned, looking at me, her eyes filled with the very same pity I wanted so desperately to avoid. "You can't just let her get away with this, you know," she said.

"I know," I replied in a flat voice. But inside, I wasn't sure.

CHAPTER TWENTY-SIX

I ran to the gear room, tears blinding my vision. I pushed open the door and made a beeline for my locker, my mind whirling with thoughts I didn't want to think. I needed an escape—a chance to lose myself for a few blissful hours. And I knew exactly how to do it. Out on the slopes, all alone, flying mindless and free.

Becca's and my lockers were next to one another. We'd planned it that way after one of the high school students had graduated two years ago, abandoning the storage space adjacent to mine. Becca had claimed it immediately, saying this way we didn't have to pause our conversation for even a moment as we collected our gear on our way out to class.

I remembered sneaking into the gear room, in the

middle of the night, just before Becca's eleventh birthday, armed with colored chalk and silk flowers, so she'd have something fun to greet her the next morning. I could practically still hear her squeals of delight as she jumped up and down and hugged me after laying eyes on my handiwork. She'd thought everyone had forgotten her birthday. But I hadn't. I never did. And Becca spent the rest of the day with silk flowers entwined in her hair.

Sighing, I grabbed my board and headed outside, trying not to think as I stomped my way up the side of the hill until I reached the top of the half-pipe. I plopped to the ground, attached my bindings to my feet, and stood up at the edge of the pipe, looking down. The last time I stood here, just before I'd met Logan, I had been paralyzed with fear. Now I wasn't so much afraid as I was sad. So very sad.

I dropped in. I rode the pipe to the bottom. Then I unstrapped my board and headed back up to the top. Up and down. Up and down. Not bothering to stop and catch my breath. Not bothering to care about style or technique as I hit each lip—harder and harder, higher and higher, until I was literally flying through the air on each and every hit.

But eventually gravity and exhaustion ganged up on

me and I hit the ground, hard, the shock of ice against bone rocking me to the core. Instead of getting up this time, I lay back, staring up at the sky, tears leaking from the corners of my eyes. Why did everything have to be so messed up? Why had everything fallen apart?

"Hey, hey! Are you all right?"

I looked up. Lost in my unhappy thoughts, I hadn't heard someone approach. Not just someone, I realized, but Logan.

I scrambled to my feet, swiping the tears from my eyes. "What are you doing here?" I asked.

"Caitlin got my number from my mom and called me," he said. "She told me everything."

I hung my head. "She shouldn't have done that," I said. "I told her to keep it a secret."

"Even from me?"

"Yes. No. I don't know." I burst into a fresh set of tears. "It's just . . . so embarrassing."

"For Becca, maybe. But you did nothing wrong."

I swallowed hard. "I thought she was my friend. My best friend. How do you do something like that to your best friend?" I knew I was babbling but found I couldn't help it.

Logan pulled me into his arms, hugging me tight. "I'm so sorry," he whispered.

"It's like I keep thinking there must be some mistake," I went on. "Like maybe Olivia was blackmailing her before all of this too, and forced her to do it."

Logan pulled away from the hug. "Lexi, I don't know . . ."

"Or maybe she was just trying to slow me down a little, you know? And she grabbed me a bit too hard?"

Logan shook his head. "Lexi, you got seriously hurt. You lost a year of your life. All because some girl—no, not just any girl—your best friend—wanted to win some stupid sporting event. And now you're making excuses for her?"

"It was an important race," I protested.

He frowned. "Let's say it was the Olympics themselves. And you were in Becca's position. All you'd have to do is pull on her jacket and you could win it all." His eyes drilled into me. "Would you do it?"

I dropped my gaze to the snowy ground. "No," I said after a moment. "Of course not." My dad had instilled in me, at an early age, that a win wasn't a win if you didn't win it fairly.

Oh, Becca . . . I broke into a fresh round of tears. *Why?*

"That's it," Logan declared. "I'm taking you to Bill's."

"What?" I looked up, startled.

"If you stay here, you're going to drive yourself crazy. You need something to get your mind off things. Something that doesn't involve dangerous sports in the dark that could injure you."

"So . . . video games?" I said hesitantly. Maybe that wasn't such a bad idea. . . .

He shook his head. "No. Singing."

And that was how, one hour later, I found myself onstage at Bill's, singing my heart out, with Lulu and Scarlet and Roland accompanying me. If my life were a movie, we would have had a sold-out house, with people screaming and cheering us on as I rocked the mic. But in real life it was a school night and last minute and so there were only a few people there, mostly concentrating on the video games, rather than the show. But it didn't matter. I was onstage. I was pouring all my anger and frustration into the music. And I was already feeling a whole lot better.

What was it Coach Basil had said? How music had healing properties? I'd had no idea how right she'd been.

I still hurt, my stomach still felt a little nauseous, but at the same time the whole thing seemed . . . less important . . . somehow. On the mountain, with my friends, snowboarding was everything. Here, it was just another thing. No more or less important than anything else.

As I finished a song and took a swig of my water, I caught Logan standing near the back of the room, watching me and smiling. I grinned back, giving him a thumbs-up.

Becca had done her worst. But I wouldn't let her defeat me. I wouldn't let her—or Olivia, or anyone else—take me down. Keep me from the sport I loved. They didn't deserve to win.

Pride comes before a fall, Olivia had said. And she'd been right. I'd fallen badly. Both physically and mentally, my golden dream twisting into a black nightmare. It was the worst thing that could have happened to me. And yet, in a weird way, it was also the best.

Before my accident all I had was snowboarding. Winning was a reason to get up in the morning, to live, to breathe, to exist. Take that away and I was nothing, no one.

Not anymore.

I stole a peek at my bandmates. At Logan in the back of the room. My accident had somehow opened up an entire universe of awesome that I had no idea existed beforehand. I felt like some horse who had worn blinders her whole life, and only now could I really see.

Sure, my father might call these things, these people, distractions, but for me they were . . . enhancements. They didn't take me away from the mountain. They made the mountain feel like home.

For the first time since I'd returned to Mountain Academy, broken and scared, I knew I wanted to stay. I wanted to keep snowboarding and maybe get back to where I had been if I could. To keep going for the gold. But if I did end up in the Olympics someday? I'd be competing as a different person than I was before the accident. One who knew Olympic glory was just one single dream. And that real life was filled with hundreds.

I grinned from ear to ear as we launched into my favorite song, my heart feeling very full. Everything was going to be okay. No, everything was going to be—

I froze as the door at the back of the coffee house opened, snow blowing in from outside. The band played on, but the words stuck in my throat, and suddenly I was unable to sing. Unable to move.

My dad stalked up to the makeshift stage, grabbing the mic from my hand.

"Come on, Alexis. We're going home."

CHAPTER TWENTY-SEVEN

My dad didn't speak to me the entire way home. Just drove up the mountain, staring out the windshield, a grim look on his face. I shifted uncomfortably in my seat, wanting to explain. Wanting him to understand why I had to be there. What had driven me there in the first place. But I wasn't ready to open up that can of worms. Once he knew what Becca had done, it would start an avalanche of inquiries and investigations that would flip my world upside down. I was finally starting to heal. The last thing I wanted was to yank off the scab and start all over again.

He parked near his staff cabin and stormed inside, not turning to see if I would follow. Half of me wanted to flee—to head back to the dorm and lock the door and ignore his calls. I didn't want to hear what he had to say. But I knew it would only prolong the inevitable. So I gave up the fantasy and slunk inside after him.

He was in the kitchen when I entered, running some kind of nasty green goop through the blender. One of his disgusting kale protein shakes, I realized. Dad's go-to when he was severely stressed out.

"So, yeah. That happened," I said, at a loss for what to say. I wanted to ask him how he knew I was there, but what did it matter, in the end? He'd found my sanctuary and dragged me away. I hadn't even gotten a chance to say good-bye to Logan. Part of me wondered if I should apologize to him, but at the same time I didn't feel very sorry. I'd done what I'd needed to do—but he would never understand that.

He didn't answer. Just poured the green slime into a tall glass and headed into the living room. I plopped down on the couch, realizing my hands were shaking. I shoved them under my thighs, watching Dad sit across from me in his easy chair, then down his gross drink in one gulp. He set the glass down on the coffee table and shook his head, making a face.

"That bad, huh?" I sighed. But I wasn't sure if I was talking about the drink.

"Maybe I was wrong to not let you spend the winter in Florida," he said at last, his voice tired and resigned. "I thought it would be good for you to come back. To feel like everything was going to be okay. But you obviously aren't ready. In fact, you don't even seem to care anymore." He paused, then added, "And if you don't care, why should I?"

I looked at him, horrified. That was so not what I was expecting him to say. "Dad. That's not—"

He waved me off. "It's all right," he said. "I get it. You don't have to apologize or make excuses to help me feel better. This is your life, Lexi. And you're allowed to live it any way you want to." He gave me a rueful smile. "You're only thirteen years old. You're allowed to change your mind about what you want for your future."

"But I haven't changed my mind," I protested. "And I *am* ready to be back, I swear!"

"Yeah? Well, you have a funny way of showing it," he said grimly. "Sneaking off to parties, meeting up with boys, going off campus, for goodness' sake, and joining a band? Lexi, any one of these things could get you expelled if you were caught. How is that caring for your future here?"

I hung my head. He made it all sound so bad. How could I explain to him it was just the opposite? That these things had helped my recovery, not hurt it.

"Dad . . ."

"Look, I've called your mother," he told me. "I've let her know the situation. I'll book you a ticket back to Florida in the morning. You can stay until Christmas break and then you can head home for the rest of the school year."

"What?" I cried. "No! No, Dad, please! You can't send me away. Not now! I've been working so hard. I'm going to rejoin my class next week. They say I'll be able to compete again really soon." My voice broke. "Look, I'm sorry. I should have told you about the whole band thing. But it's really no big deal. They're good kids. And music is very healing!"

You have to tell him, a voice inside of me nagged. *You have to tell him the whole truth or he'll never understand.*

But, try as I might, I couldn't get the words out. Couldn't bring myself to admit that I'd lied to him from the beginning. He wouldn't understand. And it would only make things worse.

It was funny. Once upon a time—and not long ago either—I would have loved to have gone back to Florida. To leave this whole nightmare behind me and start fresh. But not anymore. Not after all I'd been through, all I'd learned. I couldn't just quit now.

I couldn't let Olivia—or Becca—win.

CHAPTER TWENTY-EIGHT

Lexi! Over here! Over here!"

My eyelids felt as if they were made of lead as I scanned the cafeteria at breakfast the next morning, my stomach twisting at the strong scent of burning sausage wafting through the air. I spotted my friends, all gathered at our regular table, waving and beckoning me over with an unusual amount of enthusiasm, given the early hour. I sighed and forced my feet to move in the proper direction, feeling as if I was slogging through mud.

It wasn't surprising; I hadn't slept a wink the night before, my mind tormented and my heart aching, thinking about my new future. A future with no more snowboarding. No more singing in the band. No more Logan.

It was all too much to think about—and yet I couldn't stop the thoughts from rolling around in my head, chasing away any hope of sleep.

"Oh my gosh, Lexi! We just heard!" Brooklyn cried, interrupting my thoughts of doom and gloom. She leaned across the table, her face shining with eagerness. "I seriously cannot believe it!"

I stared at her with blank and bleary eyes, my mind madly trying to decipher her words. What was she talking about? Did she know about me going back to Florida? I knew word traveled fast at Mountain Academy, but this was ridiculous. "Um, what did you hear?"

"Oh, we heard *everything*," Jennifer butted in, a fiercely indignant scowl on her face. Then her expression softened. "Poor Lexi. I can't believe you had to go through something like that."

"You know, I always thought there was something weird about her," her twin, Jordan, added in a disdainful voice. "But I never expected her to go this far."

"Some people just can't take the pressure," Brooklyn sneered. "Pathetic, really. She must have been so jealous of you."

"Even still," Jessie chimed in, looking up from her

drawing. "Jealous or not—what she did was downright criminal."

I swallowed hard, looking from friend to friend, confused at first. Then it finally dawned on me exactly what they must have been going on about. Sure enough, I glanced down at Jessie's sketchbook and found a very realistic likeness of Becca, sporting devil's horns and goatee, with the word "CHEATER" scrawled underneath. Oh no.

"Oh. That," I muttered, my heart dropping to my knees as I slumped to my seat. Seriously, this was the last thing I wanted to deal with today, on top of everything else. "Who told you?" I asked, though I could already guess. Sometimes my roommate was far too "friendly" for her own good.

"Caitlin," Brooklyn said, sure enough. "But she was really worried about you!" she added, catching my annoyed expression. "When you disappeared last night? She thought something bad had happened to you. She was freaking out, searching the school . . ."

I sighed. Of course she was. Gossip or not, Caitlin was a good friend, and I had been so wrapped up in my own problems I didn't even stop to consider who I'd worry by taking off like I did. I should have texted her and given her a heads-up. Maybe she could have even covered for me, then, when my dad came looking.

My gaze traveled across the table, taking in all my friends' faces. I knew I should be grateful they were all so supportive. But at the same time, it was all too embarrassing. To have something so private and painful be made into such a public spectacle. Even now I could feel the stares of the other students from around the caf. Whispering excitedly about what they'd heard. *Poor Lexi. Betrayed by her best friend.*

"Guys, can we talk about something else?" I tried, hating the desperation I heard in my voice. "It's really no big deal. . . ."

"Oh, Lexi!" Jessie threw her arms around me, dragging me into a suffocating embrace. "You don't have to act all strong! You have every right to be hurt! I mean, hello? Your best friend tried to kill you!"

That was it. I squirmed out of the hug, my stomach swimming with nausea. "I've—I've got to go," I stammered, turning on my heel and fleeing the cafeteria, not caring how much attention I was bringing on myself. I just had to get out of there. Find someplace to be alone with my thoughts.

I somehow ended up in the bathroom, staring at my reflection in the smeared mirror. I looked terrible— hollow eyes, rimmed in black. Dad would have a fit if he saw me in this state. Maybe I should go back to the dorm. Skip breakfast and try to get some sleep. It wasn't as if I was hungry at this point anyway.

I was about to head out of the bathroom when a sob stopped me in my tracks. I whirled around; I hadn't realized I wasn't alone. And from the sound of it, whoever was in here with me was having just as bad a day as I was.

"Um, hello? Are you okay?" I called out, for some reason feeling the need to comfort. Maybe because I couldn't comfort myself.

The sobbing stopped abruptly, as if the person behind the door had clamped a hand over her mouth. I stood, waiting for a moment, then decided maybe she didn't want to talk about it, whatever it was. I could definitely understand that. But just as I turned to leave, I caught a glimpse of shoes under the stall door.

I gasped.

"Becca?" I called, hesitantly, though I already knew the answer. I'd recognize those worn blue Converse anywhere. We'd designed them together on the company's website, special-ordering them back when we were friends and did stuff like that.

"Go away," Becca's muffled voice begged from behind the stall door.

I frowned. "I think we should talk."

"I don't want to talk."

I crossed my arms over my chest, leaning against the counter. "Well, then I don't want to leave the bathroom."

Silence then. "What do you want from me?"

"I want to know what happened out there on the mountain."

Becca laughed bitterly. "You already know. Evidently the whole school knows."

"I didn't tell them, you know," I tried, in case it made any difference. "I wasn't going to say anything. Seriously."

"It doesn't matter," Becca replied. "I want them to know. I want everyone to know what a horrible person I am. It's what I deserve for what I did."

My heart squeezed at the raw pain I heard clear in her voice. This was my best friend, I reminded myself. I knew her better than anyone else. It didn't matter what they thought she was capable of. I knew the truth. I knew my friend.

"Look, Becca, it's not a big deal," I pleaded. "I mean, yeah, of course it is," I amended, realizing how stupid that sounded. "But I know you would never do something like that on purpose. And that's what I'm going to tell everyone, okay? It wasn't your fault. They'll have to understand. It was just an accident. It could have happened to anyone."

I paused, waiting, my breath solidifying in my throat. But no sound came from the stall.

"Becca, please!" I implored, not wanting to give up. "I love you. You're my best friend. Just tell me it was an accident and we never have to talk about it again. You don't have to avoid me and we can be friends again and you don't have to feel guilty about anything." I knew I was babbling but found I couldn't help it. "Just say something!" I blurted. "Anything! Please!"

The door slowly opened. Becca stepped out, her makeup smeared and her face stained with tears. She met my eyes with her own.

"It wasn't an accident," she said in a hoarse voice, then pushed by me and out the door.

CHAPTER TWENTY-NINE

I got the text from my father just after lunch. Requesting that I meet him at the repair hut before I headed out for my afternoon classes on the slope. With heavy feet and an even heavier heart I trudged my way through the snow, pushing open the door with reluctance.

My dad stood in the doorway, his face grave. Without a word he grabbed me and pulled me into a huge hug, practically squeezing the life out of me. I struggled at first, but the warmth of his arms after such a rotten twenty-four hours ultimately felt too good to resist. I found myself burying my face in his chest, rejoicing in his familiar Old Spice scent, allowing myself, for one blissful moment, to be a kid again—and to believe Daddy could make everything okay.

But the hug ended too soon. And things were still not okay. Dad took me by the hand and led me over to the folding chairs. Then he pushed a cup of steaming hot chocolate into my hands. Extra marshmallows, I noted dully. It was that kind of day.

"Oh, Lexi," he said, reaching over and squeezing my hand. His eyes were filled with regret. "I'm so sorry. You should have told me. I would have understood. Now it all makes sense, all your recent behavior. You must have been freaking out. And then for me to punish you . . ." He trailed off, looking anguished.

I squeezed my eyes shut. Of course. Becca's story was all over school—it was only a matter of time before the faculty got wind of it. "Dad . . ."

"You know, I blame myself," he interrupted. "I should have realized you'd never just fall on a jump like that. You're far too good to be making those kinds of mistakes. I should have known there was something else going on." He looked at me imploringly. "Why didn't you tell me, sweetheart? I could have done something. At the very least gotten that girl kicked out of school. The fact that she has gotten away with it all this time . . . Still competing. Still racking up points . . ."

I wondered, for a split second, what he'd do if I just stood up and walked out of the repair hut. I so did not want to have to deal with this. Not now. Not ever, to be honest.

"I can't imagine how you must feel," Dad continued. "To have your best friend do something like that to you? You must feel so betrayed."

I squirmed in my seat. "Things happen," I managed to say. "But really, Dad, I just want to move on and forget it."

Dad frowned. "Honey, you can't just let her get away with something like that. She has to be held accountable for what she did."

I thought of Becca in the bathroom stall, crying her eyes out. "Dad," I tried, switching tactics. "It doesn't matter. I'm going home to Florida, remember? This is all going to be over soon."

"No." Dad shook his head. "It won't be. Not as long as she's still on the mountain. I mean, what if she decided to do something like this again? To someone else? And what if something worse happens to her next victim?"

Ugh. I set down my hot chocolate, no longer in the mood to drink it. I wanted to argue that Becca had surely learned her lesson. That she would never do something like that again. But how did I know for sure? I would have said the same thing the first time around—that there was no way Becca would ever try to take me out. But she had. She'd admitted it. She'd even admitted she'd done it on purpose. And if she was willing to hurt her best friend in order to score a win, what would stop her from doing something even worse to an actual enemy?

But still, this was Becca. . . .

"There will be a disciplinary hearing tomorrow morning," my dad informed me. "The dean and the school board will be there. They want to hear exactly what happened."

I frowned. Evidently the powers that be must not have heard there was an actual video. Otherwise why bother getting testimony—they could simply see what had happened firsthand. I wondered if I should mention this little detail to my dad, but then decided against it. I needed to keep it on the down-low until I decided what to do. If they saw the video, Becca would be expelled on the spot. Her snowboarding future would be over forever. Was I really ready to go there?

"Please don't make me do this!" I begged, knowing,

even as I said the words, they would probably do no good.

Sure enough, my dad just shook his head. "I'm sorry, sweetie. But you don't have a choice. As a student of this school, you're required to go in front of the disciplinary committee and tell them the truth. If you do not, well, you're going to find yourself in as much trouble as Becca."

CHAPTER THIRTY

That evening a huge storm rolled in—the biggest, baddest nor'easter to hit Vermont in the last ten years—or so the weathermen said. It socked the resort full force all night long—wild wind, heavy snow—and when I woke up the next morning, it was still raging, the world outside my window completely lost in a whirlwind of white.

As I rolled out of bed, I found Caitlin at the window, dressed in her black flannel pajamas, peering outside. She turned to me. "Snow day!" she exclaimed, her eyes gleaming. "All classes canceled!"

I raised an eyebrow. "What about training sessions?"

Caitlin shook her head, her black braids swinging from side to side. "The lifts are closed," she informed me. "They can't run them in these kinds of winds. Not to mention they're predicting like five feet of snow. The biggest storm of the year for sure. Maybe even the decade."

"Wow. That's crazy," I said, joining her at the window, which was crusted with ice and snow. You couldn't even see the ground below. It was likely no one would be allowed out of the dorm until the storm moved on.

Which seemed fine to Caitlin, who danced over to her bed, throwing herself down and yanking the covers over her head. "I'm going to sleep until noon," she declared in a muffled voice under the blankets.

"Good idea," I agreed, heading back to my own bed. But before I could crawl in, my cell phone beeped, signaling a text. Reluctantly I grabbed it off my nightstand, groaning when I read the message.

Meeting still on. Admin building 10am.

"Something wrong?" Caitlin asked.

"They're still having the disciplinary committee meeting," I said with a sigh. "I thought it'd be canceled." All the joy I'd felt from the snowstorm immediately melted away, and a heaviness sank into my stomach.

Caitlin popped her head out from under the covers.

"Probably better to get it over with," she suggested, her voice filled with sympathy. "Right?"

"I guess so," I said, heading over to my dresser to pull out some clothes. "Though I still don't know what I'm going to say."

Caitlin shot up in bed. "You have to tell the truth, Lex," she reminded me, her eyes wide and serious. "If you lie to them, they could kick you out of school."

"Yeah, well, I'm pretty much gone regardless, thanks to my dad," I muttered as I pulled out a pair of jeans and stuck my feet in the legs. "And hey, maybe it's for the best."

"Alexis Miller!" Caitlin said in a shocked voice. "You don't mean that. I know you don't mean that."

I whirled around to face my roommate. "Don't I? I'm not so sure anymore. I mean, when I think about what this school has done to people. What it's made them do to others . . ."

"You can't blame Mountain Academy for that," Caitlin argued stubbornly. "There are going to be nasty people no matter where you go. That's just how life is. I mean, sure, maybe things are more intense here, but not everyone's like Becca or Olivia."

I hung my head. "I guess so. But . . ."

"Think of all our friends. Brooklyn, Jessie, the twins. Even Dante. Everyone supports one another. We cheer each other on. No one is trying to sabotage or tear anyone else down to get ahead."

I frowned. I knew, in my heart, she was right, as much as it pained me to admit it. "I know," I said. "I didn't mean it anyway. I'm just . . ." I glanced over at my roommate, a lump forming in my throat. "I'm just scared. I don't know what to do."

Caitlin got out of bed and headed over to me, giving me a huge hug. "I know," she said, stroking my hair. "You don't want to ruin Becca's life. But Lexi, this is as much for Becca as it is for you. What she did . . . It was obviously a cry for help. And you covering for her is not going to get her what she needs."

"I know," I said quietly, letting out a deep sigh. "I know."

And I did know. Suddenly I knew exactly what had to be done. Even if it was the last thing I wanted to do.

CHAPTER THIRTY-ONE

As soon as I stepped outside of the dorm, I realized why classes and training had been canceled. In fact, the storm was so strong it nearly knocked me over as I inched my way across campus, my mood as heavy as my feet. The cold air bit at my ears, and the gale-force wind pushed hard against me, as if trying to convince me to turn back, but still I forced myself to press on. *It's for the best*, I tried to tell myself. *For everyone—even Becca.* I said the mantra over and over again, in rhythm with my steps.

My dad was standing inside the front door of the admin building, peering out the window. He waved as he saw me approach and pushed open the door. Returning the gesture with reluctance, I trudged up the steps and through the doorway.

"Are you ready for this?" Dad asked as we walked down a long, featureless hallway on our way to Becca's hearing. He glanced down at me, and I caught the pity in his eyes. I gave a small shrug, feeling as if I was a prisoner on death row—dead girl walking to the electric chair. I tried to remind myself that it would be Becca, not me, in this case, who would fry. But that thought only made me feel worse.

"I really don't want to do this," I muttered, half to myself.

"I know." Dad reached over to squeeze my hand. "But sometimes we have to do things we don't want to—because it's the right thing to do."

I sighed deeply.

"It won't be that bad," he added in his glass-half-full voice. "You just have to go in and tell the truth."

Tell the truth. He made it sound so easy. Tell the truth and ruin another person's life. The life of my best friend. I thought of Becca, lying in the snow just a few days before, crying her eyes out because she couldn't meet her coach's expectations. Her dreams were as big as mine had ever been. And now I was going to be forced to stomp on them and crush them under my heel.

We stopped at a door at the end of the hall, and Dad gestured for me to enter. For some reason I had envisioned a courtroomlike setting—something out of a TV drama—where I'd literally have to take the stand and swear on a Bible or whatever. But as I stepped inside, I realized we were meeting in nothing more than a sparse conference room—one long wooden table flanked by red-cushioned chairs and ancient-looking teleconferencing equipment serving as a centerpiece. On the far wall there was a coffee service, complete with a bowl of fruit and a tray of muffins. But though I had eaten nothing since the night before, there was no way I could stomach any of it.

I took my seat at the far end of the table while my dad set about making himself a cup of coffee. The silence stretched on, and I twisted my hands together as I waited in agony, watching for the door to open again. I didn't know who to expect—my coaches? The school board? Maybe Moonbeam Vandermarkson himself? Who would serve as judge and jury in the case of Rebecca Montgomery v. Alexis Miller?

I didn't have to wait long. The door creaked open, and my breath caught in my throat as none other than

Becca herself stepped into the room. I swallowed hard; I hadn't realized she'd be here too, witnessing my testimony firsthand. This had suddenly gone from bad to worse.

Becca was wearing a plain black suit, and her hair was pulled back into a severe bun. Her eyes were rimmed with red, and her cheeks looked gaunt and sunken. She plopped into a chair across from me, avoiding my eyes, her parents flanking her on either side, also dressed in formal suits. Suddenly I felt a bit self-conscious about my casual red sweater and jeans. Her parents whispered to one another fiercely as Becca sat between them, staring down at her hands. The tension in the room was so thick you could cut it with a knife.

The silence stretched on, becoming more and more unbearable. I felt as if I was pulling off a Band-Aid the slowest way possible. The longer I sat there, the more my resolve was going to melt away. The more sorry I was going to feel for my best friend, sitting miserably across the room.

She needs help, too, I tried to remind myself. *I'm doing this for her.*

But even as I said the words, all I could think about was that first day in school. When Becca had bravely approached, chocolate milk in hand, sitting down next to me in the cafeteria when no one else would. Or the time in fifth grade when I'd lost a really big race and she'd made a homemade voodoo doll with a remarkable likeness to Olivia. The thing looked like a porcupine when we were done with it. And then there was the day my parents announced they were getting a divorce. Becca went and stole an entire package of my favorite Oreo cookies and a gallon of milk from the caf. We'd had a *Parent Trap* marathon and lamented that if only I'd had a twin, things could have worked out differently.

It was hard to believe that same girl I once shared milk and cookies with had tried to ruin my life.

At that moment the door opened again, and the dean of Mountain Academy, along with the school board, filed into the room, taking their seats. I squirmed in my chair. My father reached over and squeezed my hand under the table, giving me a reassuring look. Truth be told, it didn't help much.

"I think you all know why we're gathered here this morning," Dean Johnson began, pulling out a thick file folder and setting it on the table. "There have been some serious allegations made against a student that

286

relate to another student's safety. And I don't think I have to remind anyone how seriously we take safety here at Mountain Academy."

The board members all mumbled their assent.

Dean Johnson turned to Becca and her parents. "It has been alleged that your daughter deliberately sabotaged Alexis Miller during a snowboard cross event last winter, resulting in a crash that injured Miss Miller and kept her out of school for the remainder of the year."

He paused. I saw tension flicker in Becca's father's jaw. Her mother burst into tears. Becca just stared down at the table, her hands squeezed into fists.

"Rebecca has always been a model student at Mountain Academy," her father began in a defensive voice. "You can check her records. She has a clean slate. She's never once had any disciplinary action taken against her."

The school board members turned to the dean. He nodded. "It's true," he said, glancing down at the file folder in front of him. "Rebecca has never been in any trouble before. However—"

"What I want to know is why we're just hearing about this now?" Becca's mother interrupted angrily.

"This whole thing took place a year ago and it was thoroughly investigated at the time. Alexis here said it was an accident. That she fell on her own accord. So why is she suddenly changing her story?" She glared at me, her eyes filled with suspicion.

"Could it be because of Becca's newfound success?" her father suggested, his voice thick with the implication. He gave me a knowing look, and I stared back at him in horror. What was he trying to say?

The dean raised an eyebrow. "Can you elaborate on that?"

Becca's father nodded. "Look, it's no secret that my daughter was awarded a coveted place on the snowboard cross team once Miss Miller was injured. Miss Miller's spot, to be exact. She also received a bunch of new sponsors. Sponsors that might have signed with Miss Miller, if she had not been injured." He frowned and his voice took on a patronizing tone. "I think we can all imagine how hard it must be to return to school and see someone else doing so well, while you're relegated to the bottom of the pack." He gave me a pitying look. "She's always been the golden one. And to see my daughter take her place . . . well, I'm sure you can see what I'm saying here."

I stared at him, anger and shock warring for dominance. Oh, I could see what he was saying all right, but I couldn't believe he was saying it. Could he really be trying to get them all to believe that I was making this up—because I was jealous of Becca's success? I mean, her success was the reason I lied in the first place!

"How can you even say that?" I demanded, rising from my seat. I could feel my father grabbing at my hand, but I shook him off. "Becca's my best friend! I'd never sell her out like that—just to get ahead. That's crazy!"

"Lexi, sit down!" my father hissed.

I ignored him, turning to the school board. "You want to hear the truth?" I demanded. "Well, here it is. Yes, I knew someone had sabotaged me from the beginning. I thought it was Olivia Masters. And the reason I didn't tell anyone? Because I wanted to protect Becca. She won the race. She got the spot on the team. I was so proud of her. I didn't want it to be ripped away. And so I kept quiet. I said nothing so that she could continue succeeding. Because she deserved to win. At least that's what I thought at the time. . . ."

Out of the corner of my eye I could see Becca's white face. Her horrified eyes. But I found I couldn't stop. The anger I hadn't even realized was there, deep inside, was now raging like a fiery inferno. At that moment I hated Becca. I hated her for what she'd done to me. The position she'd put me in. I hated her for destroying our friendship. For taking everything from me and not even telling me what I did to deserve it.

"Becca sabotaged me," I said flatly. "She admitted it and told me it wasn't an accident. I don't know what made her do it. I don't know if I did something to make her want to destroy my life or if it was just a spur-of-the-moment act. But she grabbed my jacket. She made me fall."

I collapsed back onto my seat, exhausted, hurt, betrayed. There, I'd said it. That was all I could do, short of handing over the actual video. Which I supposed I would do, if I had to.

"You can't just take her word for it!" cried Becca's father, his voice now full of hysteria. "She's jealous! She's trying to knock out the competition. You can't let her rob my daughter of her dream of Olympic glory!"

"My dream? It's *your* dream, Dad!"

I looked up, surprised, to find Becca had risen to her feet. She stared down at her father with hatred in her eyes.

"It's *your* dream and it's always been *your* dream!" Becca cried. "And I'm sick of trying to live up to your insane expectations. Do you know what it's like? To try so hard to please you? I'm not like Lexi—I'm not a natural-born medal winner. And I never will be. But you can't accept that. You never could!"

And with that, she fled the room, the door banging shut behind her. Everyone looked at one another dumbly. Becca's father, ashen faced. Her mom crying.

Only I got out of my seat and ran after my friend.

CHAPTER THIRTY-TWO

Tears blinded my vision as I raced down the long hallway, sprinting as fast as I could after Becca. Behind me, I could hear my dad calling me back, but I ignored him, completely focused on catching up to Becca before I lost her in the storm.

Bursting through the doorway at the end of the hall, full force into the violent wind, I found myself slamming into something solid—make that someone—coming through the door in the opposite direction. As I flailed, losing my balance on the icy steps, strong hands gripped me by the shoulders, keeping me upright.

"Thanks," I cried as I planted my feet back down on the steps. "I'm sorry I—"

The words died in my throat as my eyes caught

those of my rescuer. "Logan?" I cried. "What are you doing here?"

"I drove up with my brother to pick up my mom. They've closed the mountain and the buses aren't running so she needed a ride back home." He stared down at me, a concerned look on his face. "Are you okay? Is something—"

The roar of a motor cut short his questions. My eyes jerked, just in time to see Becca jump on a nearby snowmobile and take off into the storm. Oh no. I looked back at Logan helplessly, then at the white whirlwind Becca had left in her wake.

"Becca." I gestured feebly to the vacant spot where my friend had just been. "She's upset. I'm afraid she's going to do something stupid. I have to go after her."

I pushed by him, slipping and sliding my way over to the second snowmobile. Straddling the machine, I forced myself to focus on the instrument panel in a desperate attempt to figure out how to turn it on. I could recognize the key in the ignition, but beyond that I was admittedly clueless. My pulse skittered as I looked up and out into the raging blizzard. I had to get this to work—now—or I'd lose her trail in the fog.

Suddenly a shadow crossed my vision. "Move back," Logan commanded. "I'll drive."

I let out a sigh of relief as he slid on in front of me and revved the motor. Wrapping my arms around his waist, I held on tight as the snowmobile roared to life and we took off into the blizzard. From behind me, I could hear my father calling again, begging me to come back inside, but I ignored him. I had no time to explain. No time to even grab a coat. All I could hope was he'd call the cavalry. Get the ski patrol on the mountain to help me, just in case. Though, truth be told, their chances of finding us somewhere on the massive mountainside, completely wrapped in fog, were slim to none. Which was why I couldn't lose Becca's trail.

"She went that way!" I shouted in Logan's ear, pointing into the storm. Logan nodded, steering the snowmobile in the direction of my hand, and soon we found ourselves racing up the empty mountainside, through thick snow and hard wind. My unprotected ears burned, and I had to close my eyes to keep out the snow. Thank goodness someone had left a pair of goggles on the snowmobile or Logan never would have been able to see. I buried my bare fingers into his jacket pockets, praying it wouldn't take long to catch up to Becca. With temperatures continuing to drop, one could easily lose fingers and ears to frostbite. And neither Becca nor I were wearing jackets, gloves, or hats.

As we gained elevation, the fog thickened, cutting visibility in half. My heart raced in my chest along with the roar of the snowmobile. How were we ever going to find Becca in this storm? Holding a hand over my eyes, I scanned the landscape. Finally, I recognized a faint light in the distance—snowmobile headlights—heading northwest.

"There!" I cried. "That's her. I think I know where she's going!" I shouted directions in Logan's ears, praying my instincts were right.

Logan revved the engine again, picking up speed. I held on tight as we rode up the mountain in bumpy waves. Soon we reached the top of Mesquite Way, the infamous snowboard cross course where it had all begun. The starting gates were nearly buried in snow, and the course flags had all blown over in the wind.

Then I saw it. Becca's snowmobile, parked under a tree.

"Becca!" I cried, as Logan slowed his own snowmobile

to a stop. Without pause I dove off and started running toward the vehicle, scanning the area for some sign of my friend. "Becca, where are you?"

But the wind stole my words as quickly as I spoke them. And there was no answer.

I ran back to Logan. "Do you have your cell?" I asked. I had to get a message to ski patrol—to let them know where we were. But I'd left my phone in the conference room.

He reached into his pocket and pulled his out. "No signal," he said grimly. "The storm must have knocked the cell tower out."

"Becca!" I tried again, scanning the landscape. I ran across the top of the trail, my boots filling with snow and my toes curling with cold. My ears and fingers had already lost all feeling, and the icy wind stung my cheeks and brought tears to my eyes. But still I kept searching. I wouldn't give up. I couldn't give up. Not until I found her. Not until I made sure she was safe.

"Here, Lexi. Take my coat!" Logan cried. I hadn't realized he'd come up behind me. He shoved the parka at me. I looked at it, then at him.

"But what about you?" He was only wearing a fleece jacket underneath. Which was more than I had, but still!

"I'll be fine," he assured me. "Just take it. You're turning blue."

I looked down at my hands and realized he was right. Reluctantly I allowed him to slip the jacket over my shivering frame, rejoicing in the warmth of the down wrapping around my body like a hug. Logan pulled off his hat and stuck it on my head. His hair stood straight up in crazy angles—which would have made me laugh if I wasn't ready to cry. I dug my fingers into the coat pockets and tried to flex them back to feeling. I wondered how Becca was faring out there, also completely underdressed for the weather. I needed to find her—and soon.

"You need to go get help!" I cried. "Go get the ski patrol. Let them know where we are."

"You can't stay up here by yourself," he argued. "It's too dangerous."

"I've got your coat," I reminded him. "And I'm not about to leave Becca. Please!" I begged. "I'll find her and I'll bring her over to the announcer's shack over there. There's a little battery-powered space heater for chilly race days. We'll wait for you there."

He looked as if he wanted to argue, but to his credit he only nodded his head. "Okay," he said. "I'll be back as soon as I can." His eyes locked on mine. "Be careful, Lexi."

"I will."

And with that, he leaped back on the snowmobile, revved the engine, and took off down the hill. I watched him go for a moment. Then I forced myself back to the mission at hand.

"Becca!" I cried out, stomping through the snow. "Where are you, Becca?"

"Lexi?" The wind was so strong I almost missed the small, scared voice. But then it came again. "Help me!" she whispered.

It was then that I saw her, clutching a tree, shivering uncontrollably. I ran to her, grabbing her in my arms and holding her tight. "Put your hands in your armpits," I instructed. "It'll help warm them up."

She obeyed without question, and I led her over to the announcer's shack, praying the heater was indeed inside. A moment later we were stepping through the door, closing it behind us to cut off the wind. With frozen fingers I found the heater and switched it on. Soon it began to glow red, and I allowed myself a much-needed breath.

I rummaged around the cramped shack, locating a couple of probably stale granola bars and a few heat packets stashed in a drawer. I tossed one bar and two packets at Becca. "Once you've defrosted a little, you can try a couple of these," I told her, remembering the snow-survival lessons we'd learned in school. "But too much heat too soon might aggravate any frostbite you might have." I began to yank off Logan's coat to put it around her.

"What are you doing? You'll freeze!" she protested.

"I'm okay," I assured her, but an involuntary shiver gave my lie away.

"We could share," she suggested timidly. "Remember? Like we used to for fun when we were kids?"

I nodded, dropping down beside her and slipping one arm out of Logan's coat. Becca slid up next to me, then slipped her arm into the empty sleeve. We cuddled up next to one another and were actually able to zip the coat around us. It was a little snug, but I figured our joint body heat could only help.

"Just hang in there, Becca," I instructed, cuddling close to try to warm us both up. "My friend Logan went to get help. He should be back any minute now with the ski patrol. We just have to hold on a little longer."

Becca nodded numbly. Then she turned to me, her eyes filled with tears. "I'm so sorry, Lexi," she sniffled. "To drag you out here like this . . . after everything I've already done to you." She closed her eyes, looking miserable. "I'm the worst friend ever."

I didn't say anything for a moment.

"What happened, Becca?" I asked. "You said it wasn't an accident—what does that mean? Did you do it on purpose? Did I do something to make you want to take me down?"

"It wasn't like that!" Becca protested. "I swear— it had nothing to do with you at all. You did nothing wrong, Lexi. You just wanted to win the race. You deserved to win the race." Her voice broke. "But I was so stupid. So desperate."

She broke off. I waited for a moment, then said, "Maybe you should start from the beginning."

She nodded, reaching up to brush an icy tear from her eye. The heater was kicking in, but the floor was still cold, and wisps of wind snuck in through the cracks in the walls.

"I guess it began with a conference call I had with my parents and Coach Merkin the week before," Becca said. "He told them I wasn't progressing the way I should be. That he believed I didn't have it in me to go all the way. That keeping me in school was only wasting time and money."

"Ouch." I made a face. "Why didn't you tell me that?"

She shrugged. "I wanted to," she assured me. "But you were so busy that week with your training. You were so focused—so, in the zone. I didn't want to distract you with my silly problems."

"But if I had known . . ." I trailed off, not sure what I wanted to say. If I had known, would it have made a difference? Would I have volunteered to lose the race on purpose to help Becca stay in school? Everything inside of me wanted to believe I would have. But deep inside, I wasn't so sure. After all, back then winning was everything to me. Would I have been willing to take a loss to save a friend?

"Just so you know, I didn't plan it out or anything," Becca added fervently. "Not like it makes what I did any better, but I didn't. I went into the race assuming I'd lose, like always. And then my parents would take me home and it would all be behind me. Except . . ."

She sighed. "Except by some miracle I found myself neck and neck with you and Olivia on that final jump. I guess because of all the stuff she'd been doing to sabotage you, you'd both ended up slowing down. And as we approached the jump, I had this sudden feeling like maybe I could prove everyone wrong. Maybe I could win this thing and prove to my coach and parents that I belonged here after all."

"And so you grabbed my jacket," I concluded.

"I was going to," she admitted. "But then at the last minute I changed my mind. I couldn't do that to you. You worked so hard to get where you were. And even though I was crazy jealous, I couldn't bring myself to deliberately hurt my best friend."

"But . . . the video . . ."

Her face turned bright red. "By the time I decided not to do it, it was too late. I had lost my balance, and I knocked into you by accident. That caused your fall. I know that sounds really convenient. But it's the truth. Not that I expect anyone to believe me now."

"Oh, Becca . . ."

"And then you hit that tree." She squeezed her eyes shut, obviously remembering. "Oh, Lexi, you don't know what it was like to watch that. To know it was all my fault. Because of my jealousy. My stupidity." She shook her head. "I wanted to go see you immediately," she added. "To apologize and confess everything. But I was too scared. Not only about being kicked out of school or whatever—but about you knowing what I had done."

She hung her head. "My parents were so proud, which only made it worse. We're not rich, and they've sacrificed a lot to send me here. To see the looks on their faces as they told the coach he was wrong and that I deserved to stay . . . well, I couldn't disappoint them.

"It wasn't until the next day that I learned Olivia knew what I had done. She told me if I didn't do what she said, she'd release the video, taken by one of her Boarder Barbies. I think she thought it would be funny— to have me in her club. A big slap in the face for when you came back to school. And I went along with it, like an idiot." She shook her head. "I think at that point I would have done anything in the world to keep you from finding out.

"Anyway," she said with a shrug. "Now you know

what happened. And just so you know, I don't expect you to forgive me. I don't deserve for you to forgive me. In fact, I deserve for you to hand over that video to the school board or the police or whomever you think should have it. Let them see what I did. And when they come to me, I won't deny that I did it. It doesn't matter if it was an accident in the end. I'm still responsible."

I swallowed hard. The truth was out there now, stark and undeniable. And it was still up to me to decide what to do about it. Should I turn her in? Make her answer for what she'd done? Or let her walk away—allowing her own guilt to serve as the ultimate punishment?

I didn't know. I just didn't know.

"I'm sorry, Lexi," Becca said at last. "I know that sounds stupid and lame. But I am sorry. I'm really, really sorry."

And she was. I saw that she was. She was living under a mountain of regret, feeling powerless to do anything about it. Suddenly I realized exactly what I needed to do. Drawing in a long breath, I reached into my pocket and pulled out the thumb drive.

"Take it," I said.

She stared down at the drive, then at me. "Is that . . . ?"

"It's the video," I confirmed. "I don't know for sure if it's the only one, but I took it off Olivia's computer and deleted her copy. So it's yours now. Do what you think is right to do."

CHAPTER THIRTY-THREE

Despite the storm, or maybe because of it, word had spread like wildfire, and it seemed like half of Mountain Academy was gathered at the bottom of the mountain as ski patrol escorted us to safety. It was more than a bit embarrassing to be seen being dragged down the mountain on a rescue sled once again, but the warm blankets they'd wrapped around us to keep out the chill more than made up for the humiliation factor. By the time we reached the bottom, the storm had subsided somewhat; the winds had calmed, and there was even a hint of the sun itself, shyly peeking out from behind a cloud, as if apologizing for its recent absence.

We were both taken to the ER in neighboring Paddington. I was discharged almost immediately, with just a small patch of frostbite on my right hand. When I exited, I found my dad, wearing out the waiting room floor, pacing nervously back and forth. I wondered, for a moment, if he was going to yell at me for foolishly running off into a storm like I had. But then I caught the look of relief on his face as his eyes fell on me.

"Lexi!" he cried, running over to me and grabbing me into a huge hug. He squeezed so tight he almost crushed me, but I didn't mind. "Oh, sweetie, I thought . . ." He trailed off, but I knew exactly what he couldn't say.

"What were you thinking?" he demanded, pulling away from the hug. "Just taking off in a storm like that?"

"I had to save Becca," I replied. "I couldn't just let her go."

My dad reached out, stroking my hair with his hand, smiling at me. "It was very brave of you," he said. "But foolish as well. You could have died out there."

"Becca *would* have," I reminded him. Then I drew in a breath. "Have you seen her? Is she okay?"

"From what I understand she has some severe frostbite on her right hand," he told me. "But they say she's going to be okay. They just want to keep her overnight for observation."

I let out a sigh of relief.

"Her parents are with her," my father added. "I think the three of them have a lot to talk about." He shook his head. "You kids. All this pressure you're under. You're such amazing athletes, sometimes it's hard to remember how young you really are."

"I'm not *that* young," I protested.

But he held up a hand to stop me. "Let me finish," he said. "I know you've had a tough time of it since you've been back. And I feel partially responsible for that. You told me you needed time—and yet I've been pushing you, pressuring you. In some ways, I'm no better than Becca's parents." He hung his head. "You have to understand. I was trying so hard to stay positive, to show you that I still believed in you and your dreams. Yet I never thought to ask you if you still had the dream to begin with." He gave me a rueful look. "It's your life, Lexi, not mine. You get to choose what you want to do with it."

"I want to stay," I blurted out, before I could stop myself. "I don't want to go back to Florida. I want to stay here and continue my training."

He bit his lower lip. "Lexi, are you sure? There's no

harm in taking a semester off. You'll be fine to come back next year and—"

"No," I declared. "I don't want to give up snowboarding. But I also don't want to give up singing. And I don't want to give up my new friends. Not that I won't take my training seriously—but at the end of the day there's more to life than snowboarding. And I want to do it all."

For a moment my dad was silent. I held my breath, waiting to hear what he'd say. Then his face broke out into a large grin. "All right, then," he declared. "I'll talk to the board in the morning. I'll tell them to rip up those withdrawal papers."

"And one more thing," I added, a small gleam in my eyes.

"What's that?"

"Next Saturday?" I grinned. "I want to race."

CHAPTER THIRTY-FOUR

Ladies and gentlemen! Next up in the tenth annual Vermont Snow Stars Competition at Mountain Academy, we have four very talented athletes competing in the snowboard cross event."

I rocked back and forth on my board, my fingers white-knuckling the starting handles, scarcely able to concentrate on the announcer's words, my gaze focused on the crowd around me. Once this was my favorite part of any race. The anticipation, the adrenaline surging. But now it was all I could do not to run screaming from the cage. My heart beat wildly in my chest, and my hands were shaking so hard I could barely hold on. I had to force my eyes straight ahead, so as not to look down.

"In the second stall, we have Alexis Miller, eighth-grade

freestyle rider here at the academy. Alexis is competing in her very first race since an injury knocked her out last year. Guys, let's welcome her back, okay?"

I felt my face heat as the crowd roared their approval. Soon a chant of "Golden Girl" rang through the air. Once upon a time I had loved this kind of attention. Having actual fans. But now it was kind of embarrassing. Especially with Olivia in the stall next to me.

Speaking of… I glanced over to find her staring at me.

"What?" I growled. I so did not have anything to say to her.

She rolled her eyes. "Did you really think it was me?" she asked. "All this time—did you really think *I* was the one who grabbed your jacket?"

I frowned. "I don't know. I guess."

She snorted. "Look. It's no secret I'm not your biggest fan. And sure, I'd be thrilled to have my dad off my back when it comes to you. But sorry to disappoint, Golden Girl, you're just not worth risking my career over. I don't need to resort to dirty tricks to score a win. I would much rather defeat you the old-fashioned way."

She looked so offended that I had to laugh, despite

myself. "Fine by me," I assured her. "I'm just glad to be back in the game."

And I was, I realized. I really was. Even though I was scared as anything, I was also admittedly pretty excited. To be on the mountain. Racing. There was a time I had thought I would never be here again. Whatever came of this, I was glad I had done it. That I had had the courage to try.

"And they're off in three, two, one—"

The starting pistol sounded and the gates slammed down. I threw my hips forward, forcing my gaze straight ahead as I pushed off, jolting out of the pack, the wind whipping at my face as I popped over the first few rolling hills. I kept my knees bent, my body aligned, and at first everything felt good. I even had this crazy idea that I could actually pull this off. That I actually had a chance to win.

But then, suddenly, I couldn't breathe.

The panic rushed through me, threatening to crush my ribs. Everything felt as if it was going super fast, yet, at the same time, unbearably slow. As if I were drowning underwater and couldn't make it to the surface to catch my breath.

What was I doing? I wasn't ready for this. Was I crazy to have thought I was ready for this? I was going to crash and burn and—

And sing. I was going to sing!

At first I was more than a little embarrassed, belting out the first classic-rock tune that came to my head as I raged down the mountain. What was everyone going to think? Would they assume I had lost it? That I was totally and utterly insane? But then I realized I didn't care. If this was what it was going to take to get me down to the bottom of the mountain, then this was what I was going to do.

And to my surprise, the crowd did seem to like it. In fact, I could hear a few of them actually singing along as I made my way toward the first banked turn. It made me grin, and I sang even louder, giving them a cheerful wave, while concentrating on my next move.

I was behind Olivia and one other girl, and I watched as they entered the first turn, sweeping up the side to gain speed before exiting around the bend. I followed them, doing my best to score as much altitude as possible, but I didn't make it as high as I'd hoped, and I fell a little farther behind.

But that was okay, I assured myself. The race was far from over. I forced myself to stay focused, choosing my line and readying for the first big tabletop jump. Get good air on this and maybe I could pull ahead or at least catch up.

A moment later I shot over the jump, still singing my heart out. The crowd roared as I flew through the air, the familiar rush of adrenaline seizing me as I soared. I stuck the landing perfectly and launched ahead of the other girl. I could hear her scream of annoyance as she crashed and burned behind me.

Now it was just me and Olivia. I bent my knees and tucked my body in tight, eeking out more speed. My new board responded, flying across the snow, and soon I found myself gaining ground.

We hit the next jump at the same time, popping into the air in silent flight, then arcing back down to the earth below. And we were still neck and neck around the next turn, until Olivia's board nicked a flag, and she flailed to keep her balance. I shot past her; my breath caught in my throat as I realized for the first time that I was in the lead.

That I could actually win this race.

Then I looked up and saw the next jump.

The jump.

As I raced toward it, it seemed to loom ahead of me, becoming larger and larger until it threatened to block out the sky. My heart skittered in my chest. Was it always this big? Was it always this terrifying? Suddenly visions of me losing my edge, of losing control, of slamming headfirst into a tree swarmed my consciousness, and it was all I could do to not dig my board into the snow and come to a dead stop right then and there.

But then the question above the school gates came rushing back to me.

What would you attempt to do, it asked, *if you knew you could not fail?*

I knew the answer.

I tucked down. Knees bent, board flat. I narrowed my eyes, focusing on the lip, ready to pop and soar and win this thing once and for all.

I soared through the skies.

I didn't fall.

And a moment later I crossed the finish line first.

CHAPTER THIRTY-FIVE

O h my gosh, Lexi! You were amazing! Totally amazing!"

I looked up to see Caitlin barreling toward me, arms open wide, and I had to plant my feet firmly on the ground to prevent myself from being bowled over by her enthusiasm. Brooklyn and Jessie and Jordan and Jennifer soon joined her, and a moment later we were all jumping up and down in a big group hug. Dante hovered nearby, watching us with an embarrassed smile on his face.

"Thanks, guys," I said when we finally parted, my face still flushed with excitement. "It feels good to be back!"

"Not only back, but winning!" Brooklyn reminded me. "You totally crushed them all!"

"Even Olivia!" added Jessie. "At one point I was so sure she was going to win!"

"But then you just zoomed past her!" added Caitlin, her eyes flashing her excitement. "I'd say that's a little karmic justice right there," she added with a smirk.

My hands involuntarily wrapped around the gold medal hanging from my neck, as if I was afraid it'd be taken away if I breathed wrong or something. "I'll catch up with you guys later," I told them. "And we can celebrate properly."

They all hugged me again and continued to yell their congratulations across the mountain base as I walked away, which made me smile. Not because I was proud of having won the race, but because I was lucky enough to have such good friends. As Caitlin had said, not everyone at Mountain Academy was out to win at all costs. Most were still decent kids who just loved the sport of snowboarding.

From now on, that would be me, too.

I stepped into the locker room, preparing to put away my board so I could join the others at the after-party. It was only after I closed my locker that I realized I wasn't alone. I whirled around. Becca stood in the doorway.

Her hand was still bandaged from the frostbite she'd suffered. But she was smiling.

"You were awesome out there today," she said. "Really great. I bet it'll take no time at all for you to get back to where you were."

"Yeah, maybe," I agreed with a shrug. "But if not? That's okay too. I'll be fine either way."

"Yeah," she said. "I know you will." Then she drew in a breath. "I only wish I could be around to see it."

I cocked my head in question. "What do you mean?"

She reached into her pocket and pulled out the thumb drive. "I'm going to give this to the school board," she told me. "I'm going to confess what I did, and then I'm going to withdraw from Mountain Academy. I had a long talk with my parents—they're disappointed, of course, but I think they're starting to understand. They're packing up my room now. We'll be heading back to Boston in a couple hours."

I stared at her, hardly able to believe what she was saying. "You're going to turn yourself in?" I asked. "Are you sure?" Suddenly, I realized, I didn't want her to do anything of the sort—even if that was why I'd given her the thumb drive to begin with.

I had wanted her to do the right thing.

But now I didn't want her to leave.

"It's time, Lexi," she told me. "Actually it's way past time. But it has to be done. To be honest, even knowing that I'm going to do it feels like this huge weight being lifted from my shoulders. Like I can actually breathe properly for the first time all year." She gave me a regretful look. "Thank you for letting me do it myself. You could have turned me in—you had every right to, in fact. But somehow it feels better to be able to stand on my own two feet."

"Oh, Becca," I said, my heart melting at the regret I saw on her face. This was my best friend. My brave best friend. I took a hesitant step forward, then threw my arms around her, pulling her to me. At first she felt stiff and unyielding—as if she were afraid to hug me back. But eventually she gave in, melting into my arms.

"You should hate me," she choked out as we hugged and cried together. "You should be, like, hitting me instead of hugging me."

I shook my head. "No way. We've all made mistakes. We've all fallen—in a way. But now it's time to get back up and move on. It's the only thing we can do."

EPILOGUE

Three Months Later

Ladies and gentlemen, give it up for the first-place winner of the Littleton Junior High fourth annual Battle of the Bands . . . Manic Pixie Dream Girl!"

The crowd went wild. Scarlet and Lulu and I squealed in unison, locking arms and jumping up and down—hugging each other with wild abandon. We grabbed Roland and ran onstage, accepting the absurdly large trophy presented to us by the announcer. Then we headed back to our setup and gave the crowd one last rousing victory song—Queen's "We Are the Champions." It was fitting, to say the least.

As I screamed into the microphone, my voice

echoing through the gymnasium, my eyes scanned the audience. There, at the back of the room, stood my dad, bobbing his head awkwardly to the music. I grinned and gave him an enthusiastic wave. It was funny—at first he'd been so against my singing. But since our whole heart-to-heart talk he'd become my biggest fan, even getting me special permission from the school board to travel off campus to practice once a week, as long as I kept up with my studies.

I was sweating like crazy when we finished the last number and finally managed to crawl offstage and into the packed auditorium. As I wove my way through the crowd, I was assaulted with congratulations from strangers, friends, and fellow Mountain Academy students. When Coach Basil had learned of the gig, she'd rented a bus and offered a ride to anyone who wanted to watch me sing. Pretty much the whole school had gotten on board. Even Olivia, though she claimed she just wanted to hear with her own ears how much we stunk.

But I didn't care. Because the one person I wanted to be there more than anyone else suddenly stepped into my line of sight. As sweaty from dancing as I was from singing. And just as happy.

"Becca!" I cried, waving my hands wildly to get her attention.

"Lexi! That was amazing!" she squealed as she bounced over to me. "I just knew you guys were going to win the second you got onstage. You totally blew everyone else away."

"Thanks," I said, accepting her congratulatory hug. "It was pretty awesome, I have to admit."

Becca shook her head proudly. "On the slopes and onstage. You truly are a golden girl," she teased.

"Yeah, yeah." I waved her off, but inside I was dancing.

I hadn't seen Becca since the day of the race three months ago, when she came to my dorm room to say good-bye. Her meeting with the school board had gone as well as could be expected, she'd told me. They'd accepted her resignation and thanked her for being brave enough to come forward.

"So how have you been?" I asked, looking her over. "Do you like your new school?"

"I love it," she replied. "It's actually refreshing to have friends who have no ambition whatsoever." She laughed.

"As long as you don't start joining them." I gave her a wink.

"Please. I could never," Becca assured me. "In fact, I already have a huge thing lined up, I'll have you know."

"Oh?"

"Girl's hockey!" she exclaimed. "They have this league in my hometown. It's so much fun. You know I've always been into team sports. But with my schedule here I never got a chance to play much. But I tried out and somehow I made the team. I'm going to be their new goalie."

"That's awesome!" I cried. I raised my hand to give her a fist bump. "I can't wait to see you play!"

We talked a little more and then hugged and parted ways. Becca's parents were waiting outside to drive her back home. I felt the tears spring to my eyes as we said good-bye. But I knew it was for the best. After all, she had her own dreams to follow.

And I had mine. As I watched her go, I felt a hand on my shoulder. I whirled around to see Logan standing behind me, a big grin on his face.

"You were amazing," he said. "But you already know that, don't you?" He reached over and pulled me into a sweaty hug.

"No more amazing than you," I reminded him. "After all, I'm not the only one who scored a win today."

Logan had also competed that morning—on the slopes, that was—and managed to walk away with first place on the half-pipe. A first place that came with a season pass to Green Mountain, I might add. Meaning no more dead-of-night stealth snowboarding. We could ride together anytime we liked.

Logan blushed. "Yeah, that was pretty cool," he admitted. "I was glad my mom could be there to see it, too."

"You should have seen her face," I exclaimed. "She was so proud." I grinned. "Who knows? Maybe someday we'll both be up there on that podium, winning Olympic gold."

"Maybe so," he said. "Or maybe you'll win a Grammy someday."

"Ooh. That'd be cool," I agreed. "Or maybe a Nobel Peace Prize? Or a Pulitzer?"

"What about an Emmy? Or at least a Golden Globe?"

I laughed. "How about all of the above?"

"Why not?" he declared. "I mean what is that saying above your school again? 'What would you attempt to do if you knew you could not fail?'"

"Oh, I know very well I can fail," I said with a laugh. "But that doesn't mean I'm going to stop attempting anytime soon—whether it's on or off the slopes."

"I know you won't," he assured me. "And for that— no matter what happens—you'll always be a golden girl to me."